I0664374

Inauguration Day

2013

Bernard (Frank)Fernandez

BeachHouse Books

Chesterfield Missouri USA

Inauguration Day 2013, copyright by Bernard (Frank) Fernandez, 2012.

All rights reserved.

All rights reserved, including the right of reproduction in whole or in part in any form. This novel is a work of satyrical fiction. Names, characters, places and incidents are either the product of the author's imagination or are used fictitiously. Any resemblance to actual persons living or dead or actual events should not be taken to represent any actual persons or events.

Cover Design by Dr. Bud Banis, based on a photograph of the presidential inauguration in 2005, with lettering enhanced by Dr. Banis

ISBN 9781596300828 paperback edition

Published in 2012 by

BeachHouse Books

Chesterfield Missouri USA

www.beachhousebooks.com

2013

CHAPTER 1

At 10:23 am on Thursday, April 5th, 2012, Patricia Reinhardt placed a call to Sam Saviur, the premier consumer advocate of America. This call was the first in a series of events that would change American politics forever. Ms. Reinhardt had recently sent shock waves through the nations capital by announcing that she would not seek re-election as Wyoming's Junior Republican Senator. She also indicated she was leaving the Republican party to become an independent.

"Hello, this is Sam Saviur."

"Good morning, Mr. Saviur, Patricia Reinhardt here. Even though you've only shown casual interest in seeking political office I'd like to meet with you as soon as possible to discuss the subject."

Sam's incredible mind, conditioned over the years to fasten then react immediately to impressions received, began to form a response confirming Patricia's appraisal of his attitude toward things political. Then, microseconds before the words a 'What's going on here?' signal flashed. Even factoring in her recent, sensational resignation from the Republican party, why would the daughter of the wealthy David Reinhardt want to talk with him about political office? Her family background and political positions would seem to align her with big business, his constant adversary. Uncharacteristically then, he

1

offered "Based on past experience you can understand my hesitation regarding overtures from attractive women."

"Thank you, I think. I do understand. The number that General Motors tried on you was bad news, to put it mildly. Let me assure you Mr. Saviur, I represent only Patricia Reinhardt. You and I are the only individuals who know about this call."

Patricia's response surprised and impressed Sam. She had done her homework. The G.M. incident had taken place early in his career. He had written a book criticizing one of their cars. Unable to find anything in his personal life to discredit him, they tried, unsuccessfully, to set him up by using the lure of a pretty woman.

Sam's curiosity combined with his awareness of Patricia's stunning physical attributes prompted him to say, "I can be in your office at 10:00 a.m. on April 22nd. Meeting there would generate less media attention than my office or a public place, what do you think?

"Time frame's good and I agree about the media. Thanks. Look forward to seeing you."

Patricia hung up before Sam could say goodbye. She then leaned forward in her chair, put her elbows on the desk, cradled her chin in her hands and asked herself out loud "Dear God, what have I done?"

Now that the plan had moved from the privacy of her mind to the action of the first step, she thought of the biggest negative of what she had just started, the reaction of her father, David. His contributions to the thought processes bringing about the conception of her plan were the height of irony.

CHAPTER 2

While there are those who are precocious in music, academics and athletics, etc., Patricia was precocious with regard to the human condition. From the age of nine she was an insatiable people watcher. An alert and bright child, she wanted to know what they were really thinking and feeling about their lives. She was always asking questions. As often as not, these questions went unanswered since her targets, particularly the older ones were surprised of miffed at being questioned by someone so young.

When her father asked her about this curiosity, Patricia said she wanted to learn as much as possible about people. When he asked why, she said, "Because some day I'd like to help them".

This ongoing interest in people precluded the possibility of preoccupation with relationships, or for that matter, with herself.

By her early teens, Patricia began to receive impressions of the movers and shakers of America. There was a constant stream of important visitors to the Reinhardt ranch, and they were some of the biggest players in business, government and education. Politicians and educators were interested in David's fundraising capabilities. Businessmen were always trying to tap in to his access to capital as well as seeking his highly regarded counsel regarding their corporate strategies.

Because she so wanted to be favorably impressed, Patricia found it difficult to comprehend what she had heard from these men. Their insensitivity to everything except their own self interest was clear. They couldn't have cared less about the people they served be they stockholders, constituents or students. They were clever enough, however, to provide the perception of caring so they could receive the support required to stay in power.

Additionally, there could be little question that they would employ whatever means necessary to reach their goals. Integrity did not count for much. Patricia was particularly disturbed by the educators. She had hoped they would have a genuine concern for their students but was dismayed to find their mindset no different from the business leaders and politicians.

While having dinner at their favorite restaurant, Patricia told her father about her impressions and asked for his thoughts. It took David less than five minutes to tell of his complete agreement with her assessment.

Having offered a sweeping, damning indictment of practically everyone under their scrutiny, he then proceeded to another dimension by saying this evaluation was the "good news". The "bad news" was the fact that these people were allowed to stay in their positions because of the inability of the American people to bring about meaningful change. They, alone, had this power.

By now, David had raised a good head of steam. "Let's look at our national government. I'm sick and tired of those clowns in Washington referring to "the people" as if they mean anything except to help them stay in office. As a matter of fact, we don't have a real answer to the political identity of so many Americans. About fifty percent of those eligible vote in presidential elections. Less than fifty percent vote in congressional, state and local elections so it's safe to say there are close to eighty million American voters who don't participate."

At that point, Patricia offered, "Wouldn't it be nice if we could get all those millions involved and more importantly that they cast their votes on the basis of logic, reason and a clear understanding of issues put forth by honest, intelligent individuals who cared as much about their country as their personal interests?"

David smiled; his mood instantly brightened by his daughter's noble words and said, "Yes, dear heart, it would not only be nice it would be stupendous. Let's switch gears and talk about you. I've been a little concerned about that 'birds and bees' talk we had a little while back".

"Why?"

"I don't hear the phone ringing off the hook and I'm wondering if you took my warning too seriously."

"I haven't taken any particular action to ward off those 'testosterone fueled' advances you spoke of. They just haven't happened and I'm not sure as to why."

David smiled, "I can take a pretty good run at an explanation. In addition to being an absolute knockout you've developed facially and body wise well beyond your years. Most young boys are intimidated by such physical characteristics. They believe anyone that outstanding is approached so often by so many people they wouldn't have a chance. Factor in your straight on, direct attitude, plus a self assurance I don't see in people much older than you and I'm not surprised at what you've said."

"You sure have a way of making me feel good about myself. I've learned a lot from talking to the girls along with listening when we're in a group. Most of those who are sexually active don't seem to be enjoying it and I get the impression that many of them 'go' to please their partners thereby insuring the continuance of the relationship. I can tell you right now, my self respect, and you've taught me a lot on that subject, wouldn't allow me to practice what I'm hearing. I know I sound like a snob but I don't have much interest in close friendships with boys or girls. Friendships imply regular communication. Based on a very high number of examples, I can anticipate just about everything my contemporaries are going to say. I want to be challenged intellectually and even my teachers aren't much help in that area."

David's eyes grew misty listening to his daughter. Though they had engaged in countless conversations over the years he always marveled anew at her insights, vocabulary, how articulate she was and the depth of character she revealed. His wife had died of cancer when Patricia was six leaving him as the main influence in her life. He had tried very hard to be a good one. It naturally followed that he was gratified and relieved by any indications she was developing into the fine person he so wanted her to be. David reached across the table, took both of Patricia's hands in his, then said, "O.K., now let's get serious. What sounds good for dessert?"

CHAPTER 3

By the time she graduated from high school, Patricia knew she wanted to go into government. Her motivation was simple. Since she really cared about people and wanted to help as many of them as possible she felt that participation in the governmental process was the best way to accomplish her goal.

Having set her eyes on political office, Patricia became totally committed. From her freshman year at BYU until graduating from Harvard law School she threw everything into her work. Her rewards were consistently high academic rankings.

Her summers were spent working in the offices of the most prestigious law firm in Rawlins, Wyoming. In election years she labored in the political campaigns of Republicans seeking various local and state offices. After passing the State Bar Exam on her first try, she began her own practice in Rawlins. She continued to set the stage of entering politics by becoming involved in numerous civic endeavors. This gave her a great deal of favorable exposure as well as personal satisfaction. She also kept working in political campaigns. When she wasn't occupied in those areas she was dispensing legal advice from her small downtown office for low, unheard of rates. The town's legal community didn't know what to make of her. During this period she lived in her own apartment at the Reinhardt ranch.

Two years after her return to Rawlins she became the town's first woman Mayor. Two years later she ran successfully for State Representative from Wyoming's thirty-third district. Three years later, when the incumbent's career came crashing down as the result of a very messy extra-marital affair, Patricia decided to try for the highest office she believed possible for her, the United States Senate.

With the help of many of the people she had met along the way, with her outstanding record as Mayor and Representative and with the backing of her father and his influential friends, she became U.S. Senator Patricia Reinhardt, Republican, at thirty and three months of age, the youngest Senator in fifty years.

CHAPTER 4

When Patricia thought of her father and his reaction to her future activities, she had serious second thoughts about her brainstorm. It was such a long shot and so many things had to fall into place for it to work. Maybe she should have tried to develop more seniority in the Senate and do what she could within the existing political structure. Wouldn't that be enough of a contribution to American society?

One very large reason, indicating negative, immediately came up on her mind's screen: As long as she believed there was a chance to do more, a lot more, she had to give it a try. In terms of positive impact on a maximum number of Americans, Patricia was surprised and disappointed in not being able to anticipate the limits of what she could accomplish as a U.S. Senator. She knew her evaluation of these limits couldn't be based on the very short time she had been in office so she carefully studied the accomplishments of Senators who had been around a long time. She then optimistically, calculated what she could do in two or three terms and the answer was disappointing.

After analyzing why she couldn't anticipate these limits the reason was simple and clear: She had been so engrossed in the process of reaching the highest office she believed possible, she had not given any time or energy to the specifics of what she would do when she arrived. Even with these limits she might have stayed in the Senate, at least for a while longer were it not for the 'Pygmy Factor' among so many of her colleagues. Instead of the 'Men to match our mountains' put forth by Kipling, all Patricia saw, with just the very few exceptions, were 'Men to match our ant hills'.

The almost total lack of intellectual integrity, the small minded, self serving, petty, blame someone else mentality that she and her father had defined long ago was a constant source of disappointment. These characteristics were exemplified in the squabble over the national debt limit that almost resulted in a shutdown of the government. Examination of her party's candidates for President present or gone was hardly a source of comfort. The fellow from Texas didn't warrant comment, the same could be said for the lady from Minnesota, the pizza man, the guy from Pennsylvania and the most mind boggling of all, the resurrected Knute Ginrich. As for the leader in delegate count, Mitten Konmey, Patricia had never seen a person, in or out of politics who looked so uncomfortable. That was the kindest opinion she could offer.

Though it was a minor irritant, she was also aware of a high degree of patronizing on the part of her male colleagues. Her father's explanation indicated that what would have been normal in this area was compounded by the effect of her physical attributes and her overall sense of self. None of the male senators had ever dealt with a colleague possessing Patricia's devastating mixture of beauty, sex appeal and a direct manner devoid of any affectation. Because they were so ill at ease in her presence, they were overly careful in their choice of words, stiff and studied in their expressions.

When trying to decide on an acceptable alternative to serving as Senator, she considered her longstanding belief that simplicity could be very helpful when solving a problem, ergo: If it would take too long to accomplish too little as a U.S. Senator in causing positive impact on the American people, what is an alternative? Answer – operate at a higher level. If certain activities of both parties are depressing, tell the American public why you are affected in this manner. If you can't stand the lack of courage, intellectual integrity and overall lack of character in those around you, get into as powerful a position as possible where you can do battle with these people. Hopefully, higher standards would result.

She had decided, after reviewing her analysis, why shouldn't she raise more than a little hell by taking a run at her unprecedented idea? If she succeeded, a historic, beneficial impression could be made on America in a very broad sense. Even if she failed, there would be a positive effect on the election process of this great country.

CHAPTER 5

When Sam reflected on his brief conversation with Patricia, he shook his head in mild disgust. *Curiosity is definitely not your main motivation in going to see her, Samuel. It's there, but at best, forty percent. Sixty percent is the fact that she's the most exciting woman you've ever seen.* Though his observations were limited to her appearances on television, her physical makeup combined with her candor, intelligence and what appeared to be a high degree of integrity rang a lot of Sam's bells. He couldn't help but wonder, after all the years of living like a monk, isn't it a little late to allow such distractions? Whatever the mixture of motivations, Sam didn't regret his agreeing to meet Patricia. As was his custom, he then decided he had given the matter enough time and went back to work.

On their meeting day, Sam presented himself to Patricia's secretary within seconds of the 10:00 a.m. appointment time. Thirty seconds after being notified of his arrival, Patricia opened her office door and held out her hand in welcome. She had anticipated his arriving on time and made sure she would not be on the phone. She also had informed her secretary that their meeting wasn't to be interrupted. Patricia had the impression that Sam's time utilization was extraordinary and felt an obligation to do her best in making every minute of their meeting productive.

Sam had given himself a lecture on his initial, in person reaction to this improbable woman. That he should regard her as he would any other human being. Her presence rendered any such approach inoperable. Happily for Sam, Patricia, after initial eye contact and a firm, quick handshake, immediately turned from him and with a swirl of her light summer dress led him into her office. Only Patricia's secretary saw him stumble over the slightly raised door step, his eyes locked on the shimmering figure walking ahead of him. Patricia turned and nodded toward a bright, flowery sofa. "Please sit down".

She then settled into a comfortable looking rocking chair some three feet away. Patricia's initial impression of Sam made her uncomfortable. In a very simple, direct manner he projected an intensity, a sense of purpose that caused her to feel guilty for taking his time. This feeling was new and she wondered why she felt this way about this thin, tall, graying man. It followed logically that she would begin their conversation by saying, "Thank you for taking time from what must be a very tight schedule."

Before Sam could respond, she lurched onward. "Here's why I believe you should make a serious run for political office. Based on what I know about you, the sole purpose of your existence is to help American consumers; to protect them from the shenanigans of those providing goods and services. Just as important is your monitoring any government activities that affect the people of America. I know that's oversimplified but it's good enough for where I'm going. While I'm in total agreement with your basic premise and admire your considerable accomplishments, you must be frustrated by how difficult and slow it is to travel the road you've chosen. For example, Detroit finally moved on air bags some twenty years after you started calling for them. I

14

remember Iacola and those never ending commercials. He made it sound as if they were his idea in the first place. If there's one thing I can't stand it's hypocrisy."

Sam could not abide small talk. He preferred to the point, efficient communication and usually had to set the tone of his conversations. Rarely did he meet anyone who shared this concept, someone who could so adeptly practice it. And he had never experienced it with a politician.

While Sam had heard and assimilated every word she said, he gave no response. She had not said enough. He was finally making progress in dealing with her physical charms. Someone once told him that looking at the space between a person's eyes served the same purpose as direct eye contact. For the first time he tried it and thereby escaped most of the devastating impact of her large, wide set, liquid brown eyes. It also reduced to his peripheral vision, the rise and fall of her magnificent bosom, the luxurious, reddish brown hair falling softly to her shoulders, her almost too generous mouth and the most appealing gossamer encased knees he had ever seen. Knees?

Sam hoped his face didn't betray the continuing shock and disgust he felt for himself. What's happening here? You're acting like a teenager. It isn't as if you haven't been in the company of attractive women from time to time. That aside, you've always been more interested in the subject matter of meetings. When Sam extended his appraisal of Patricia's impact he decided there were, in addition to her physical makeup, two other important dimensions to her appeal. She had a sense of self that allowed her to project the impression that she was totally at ease and comfortable with being Patricia Reinhardt. Finally, there was a look of innocence about her.

Patricia continued, "Putting it on a personal level, the most important reason for you seriously considering what I have in mind is a dramatic improvement in the timetable of what you're doing, along with increasing the scope several times over."

"What do you have in mind?"

"You're running as an independent for President of the United States in 2012."

Sam was surprised to hear Patricia say this but his face didn't register it since he was still intent on staring at the space between her eyes. He began to answer, "In the interest of conserving our time while still giving us what we want from this meeting….."

Sam's passiveness and an increasingly apprehensive attitude on Patricia's part caused her to interrupt, "Why did you come here today?"

"I was puzzled by an overture or should I say request from someone whose political and personal background differs so much from my own. Also, I find you to be a fascinating enigma. If you want you can refer to the latter as plain old man-woman stuff and I'm sure that's some of it but I'd like to think I'm also interested in the rare existence within one person of a superior intellect, dazzling persona and a high degree of integrity."

Patricia had trouble dealing with Sam's answer. No one, male or female, had ever said anything like that to her. Additionally, Sam's words had the tone of scientific opinion along with complete conviction.

16

"Thanks for the kind words and please excuse the interruption."

"I was going to give you my reasons for not being interested in public office and then ask a couple of questions. By temperament, demeanor, beliefs, attitude and probably more, I'm not suited to the process of obtaining political office. If by some miracle I were elected, the same evaluation applies to successfully executing the requisites of that office."

"My last two comments would seem to justify your using the word 'serious' when we began our conversation. As you know, I've actually declared as a candidate for president on more than one occasion. None of them could be called serious since my reasons for not being really interested in public office are real."

"Why did you do it?"

"A break down in discipline brought on by frustration from the slow rate of accomplishment."

"Having gone through the process you speak of, I can understand and relate to what you're saying. If we take a shot at this thing, you would never have to do or say anything you didn't believe. Also, you would be subjected to a small fraction of the baloney a person goes through in the course of a campaign and in the conduct of the office if elected. I realize what I'm saying is long on promise and short on specifics but I can fully support whatever I represent to you."

"Go."

"In recent years, candidates for public office have increasingly described themselves as 'outsiders' who would change what the 'insiders' were doing. Once inside their pledges prove meaningless. Also, there has been increasing criticism of our governmental system.

17

I don't believe there's anything wrong with our system of government. The problem lies with the people of the congress and the executive branch along with lobbyists and special interests engaging in the game of politics, circa 2012."

Patricia paused for a moment, then, "I don't have to give you my dissertation on politics, do I? I would think we're on exactly the same wavelength with that one."

Sam nodded and said, "Yes, we are, without question."

This response was the first indication to both Sam and Patricia of how simpatico they were in their views. "I'm flat out suggesting that we would not play politics. You would be the same person you are right now, basing all of your efforts on what's best for the people of America. Your beliefs and values would not change."

Patricia's words so surprised Sam that her presence, for the first time, became secondary to his thought processes, "Why me?"

"The foundation of my premise is integrity, more specifically, intellectual integrity. I don't know of anyone, in public or private life, who possesses the intellectual integrity you have and your motivation is exactly what I'm looking for. You've proven beyond doubt you want to help the people of this country. Perhaps as important, I've never known of any desire on your part for power or monetary gain. Two more positives: You're very articulate and your work ethic is outstanding."

"Excuse me for interrupting but I'd like to offer a few thoughts on integrity. The very important moral issues involved have never been a primary motivation for my actions and values. I figured out a long time ago that it's very smart to play it straight. Let's look at business. If you're talking long term and in most cases you should be, going my way is the best way. I could sit in a room with the best and brightest from the highest ranked business schools in the country and prove my premise. It's not well known and my corporate 'friends' would just as soon it wasn't known at all, but I startd and operated a small business a long time ago. Because I treated my employees fairly, the turnover rate was miniscule and their productivity was sensational. By treating the customers in the same way there was rapid growth just through satisfied customers spreading the word. Fair in terms of the customer meant a good product at a very competitive price."

"Interesting…now, getting back to my version of your qualifications. You obviously know and understand American business. To those who don't know what you really stand for and of course to your adversaries, you are an enemy of business. I don't see it that way. I see you as pro-consumer rather than anti-business. The attitude of the politicians in Washington toward American business can only be explained as follows: Because of their lack of intellectual integrity they won't face that same syndrome in the business world or they're not smart enough to see through the smoke screen that business lays down. Maybe it's some of both, plus their ongoing need for large amounts of money to finance' their political effort.

I have no doubt you clearly understand that the success of American business is critical to the success of our country. You just won't buy into their achieving this success at too high a cost to the American people. By too high a cost, I mean the safety and health of present and future generations. Finally, you've dealt with all of the various governmental processes here in Washington for most of your adult life. How many presidents in the last forty years come close to that profile?"

Sam didn't know what to make of what he had just heard. He was always so involved in his work, he never paid much attention to himself or what others thought of him. As a matter of fact, he wasn't doing too well in coping with this meeting, period. The combination of Patricia's personal impact plus the subject matter placed him in a position that caused him to be less than comfortable and it had a negative effect on the clarity of his thought processes. Still, he had the presence of mind to complete the information required for understanding the proposition being offered, "Why are you doing this?"

"Because I truly want to help the American people and I faced the same frustrations along with slow and limited opportunities for accomplishment in the Senate as I mentioned a little earlier with reference to your activities."

"Why don't you go for it?" Sam asked.

"In my opinion, this country's some years away from electing a woman President. The campaign I envision is going to be controversial enough without adding that factor."

"Please describe your function in this project."

"I would be the architect and the head of the campaign. It's the only way I can deliver on the promises I've made to you. Also, since I know the whole plan so well, it would be easier for me to run things than to keep explaining it to someone else. If our campaign is successful I want to be the most unusual Vice President ever. If you were to relate it to business, you'd be the Chairman and CEO and I'd be next in the chain of command, functionally, not figuratively."

Sam's comfort factor continued to deteriorate causing him to ask, "Why do you believe that someone who has never held political office would have a chance to succeed in what you're proposing?"

This remark indicated far more positive interest than he was feeling. If he had been making progress in dealing with Patricia's presence, what happened next set him back a thousand light years. Patricia knew that Sam had to be on board if her plan had any chance to fly. This fact combined with her feeling that his participating was the longest of long shots caused a level of unusual tension. To her, Sam's last question was the first clear signal of real interest on his part and she reacted with physical actions typical of her since childhood. She jumped from her rocking chair, took a few steps toward the window, raised her arms high above her head, stretched and arched backward. Mercifully for Sam she was turned away from him but then she leaned forward and effortlessly put her hands flat on the floor thereby providing a flash of thigh and the outline of a very impressive posterior. Finally, she turned toward him, smiling and projecting vibrant, top of the line health as she tossed her hair away from the back of her neck with both hands. Her smile revealed even white teeth that fit her mouth perfectly and served to intensify the brilliance of her eyes. Sam almost flinched physically.

When she realized what she had done she said, "Please excuse my school girl behavior. This thing has me wound pretty tight and I just had a feeling for the first time that you might really be interested."

Over the years, Sam had learned that putting forth his thoughts in a straight forward, truthful manner was the best way to communicate. In spite of his discomfort, he was able to reaffirm this approach and thereby surprised Patricia by saying, "The past several minutes have been extraordinary for me in many respects. I can only say there is enough interest on my part to continue this conversation within the next two or three days. If you agree, I'll call and suggest a time and place."

Since Patricia hadn't the foggiest on Sam's state of mind, she was puzzled at his abrupt termination of their meeting but still hopeful enough to quickly respond. "I'll give you my private line and cell numbers. Look forward to your call."

With that she went to her desk and wrote both numbers on the back of one of her calling cards. She then walked toward Sam who was standing in front of the couch, handed him the card, extended her hand and said, "It's been a pleasure." Sam shook Patricia's hand, smiled and said, "Same here." He then walked out of the room saying goodbye to Patricia's secretary as he passed through the outer office.

CHAPTER 6

Sam stepped from the air-conditioned comfort of the Senate office building into a Washington day of heat and high humidity. He started to hail a taxi to go back to his office, then lowered his arm and began to walk. Thinking...Why are you walking the sidewalks of Washington, Saviur? When people are faced with an important decision in the movies, they always seem to find an ocean to walk beside. The least you can do is take your usual route when you walk in Washington....from the Capitol down the tidal basin to the Washington Monument, the Jefferson and Lincoln Memorials, then the White House. Who are you kidding anyway? Barring some very important reason you haven't figured on and subject to all the details making sense, you're going to go and you know it. Don't put sugar on why. As is usually the case in such situations it's a combination of reasons. You're more than a little weary of inching along on your tired old white horse wondering how much of a difference you can really make, even if you are able to continue for another twenty years. At 65 you can't maintain the pace of ten years ago. What will it be like at 70? Who knows how many productive years are left? Your mother's recent passing was the most telling reminder you've ever received regarding your own mortality. Everyone's got to go sometime, Sam. Even if you get what those crummy insurance companies calculate, time seems to be going awfully fast these days.

Anyway, with my living habits regarding food intake and rest, I'm doing my best to prove those guys wrong and go quicker. On the other hand, who has ever taken better care of herself than dear Mom, only to develop that massive malignancy. Then we find out a couple of other family members died under similar circumstances. Plenty of ammo to develop into a full-blown hypochondriac, Samuel. Especially, since you have believed for so long in genetics as the basis for much of our physical and mental makeup. O.K., so reason number one: If you're successful, you can step up the time table on what you're trying to accomplish. Didn't Patricia say that? About this woman, am I doing a number on myself or does she really represent more beauty, truth and innocence than I've ever seen in a person her age? Hell, for that matter, any age. Of course she drives your thermostat off if the wall. If she didn't you should go see a doctor.

But I don't think I'm rationalizing when I say I'm as knocked out by these qualities as I am by what she does to my lust factor. Reason number two: Based on what I know right now, what a kick it would be to work with Patricia! Number three: What's the worst that could happen? We'd fall flat on our faces, fail miserably and I'd go back to business as usual. It probably wouldn't harm my current effectiveness. The general consensus would say I'm just not cut out for politics and these days that opinion could be taken as a compliment.

By this time he was in front of the White House. With sweat-stained shirt, his jacket slung over one shoulder, Sam stood there among several tourists and marveled at the change that had taken place in his outlook in such a short period of time. From looking with disdain on all aspects of the political process to wondering, should lightning strike, how he could ever be comfortable living in that beautiful but very large house. At that moment he wasn't thinking about the trappings of the Presidency; he was concerned with the day to day physical characteristics of actually living there. What a transition! From a small efficiency apartment almost submerged in books and files to THAT. Interestingly, Sam didn't feel at all presumptuous in considering the possibility. After all, wasn't this America where anyone could be President? As he started to continue his walk, one of the tourists, a heavyset, pleasant-faced woman said to him in a southern accent, "Sir, haven't I seen you on TV?"

"That's possible." He extended his hand and said, "I'm Sam Saviur."

The woman's face didn't register recognition. She took Sam's hand briefly, mumbled something he couldn't understand and turned back to her family. Sam smiled and continued his walk. Several blocks later he looked at his watch which indicated 12:00 noon. Even though he wasn't hungry he decided to take care of lunch. Seven minutes from the time he entered the White Castle, he walked out having inhaled four of their famous little hamburgers plus a medium Pepsi. He wondered if he had a death wish.

CHAPTER 7

They say the Kenai Peninsula in Alaska provides some of the world's greatest trout fishing. Lee Iacola, former chairman of Chrysler and Richard Davis, former chairman of Standard Oil had decided to verify this. Long time friends, they had been transported by seaplane to a remote lake accompanied by an all-purpose utility man.

Thirty minutes after landing, the two recent titans of industry were engaged in almost constant action from a boat some thirty yards from shore. One hour later, having caught and returned to the lake some eighteen magnificent fish, they did keep one for supper, the two men leaned back in the outsized skiff, lit up their imported Havana cigars and began to talk. It was an improbable conversation, perhaps inspired by the pristine, staggering beauty of their surroundings. Out of a clear blue Alaskan sky the oil man said, "Ever give much thought to squashing that seventy miles per gallon technology?"

"Hell, no. Once I've done something I let it alone. If I second guessed just half of the important business decisions I've made in a lifetime, I'd be on the funny farm long before now. On that particular decision though, it's easy to credit our friendship for a good part of my motivation. Have you ever figured what it would have cost your company if we'd gone ahead with it?"

"No, but you don't have to be a CPA to understand we're talking major, major bucks. Certainly enough to get our stockholders more than a little crazy. Would you ever use your influence to have present management reconsider the situation?"

"Nope. The changeover cost, assuming they could get the damn thing to work would be horrendous and they're having a tough enough time as it is. Before long, you will be hearing about a "Concept Car" from Chrysler that will be very fuel-efficient. Who knows when or for that matter if it will ever go into production? Personally, I think it's a P. R. ploy.

Now that I'm on my soapbox, let me respond to a question you're about to ask, i.e., what about the consumer? I only saw consumers as faceless individuals who bought our cars. I couldn't afford to give a damn about them as people. The minute I started doing that my competitors, particularly our Oriental friends, would have me for lunch.

On a related subject, screw the environmentalists and their hot house effect or whatever they call it. I'll be long gone before what they say is going to happen, happens. As far as reducing our consumption of finite fossil fuels are concerned, that wasn't my problem either. Let those gutless wonders in Washington worry about it. They were so easy to snow it was pathetic. All they gave a damn about was being re-elected. I was never turned down when I asked them to go easy on emission standards or MPG's. All me and those other guys in Detroit had to do was plead financial hardship with resulting negative effects on the economy and their campaign financing and the ball game's over. I'm playing poker with those guys, I'm bluffing four out of five times. But enough of that stuff, we're here to relax and enjoy. Let's get this beauty to the cabin for cleaning and cooking."

Davis started to say, "One more question while I'm getting a load off my chest ....."

"Enough already. I'm starting to think you're taking seriously that crap Chevron's been putting out in its advertising."

"Which one are you referring to?"

"You know, the one that has some jerk in the woods saying in a hushed voice 'Do some people care? Some people do!' as little animals are running around. What is it with you? You never used to talk like this."

The oil man just shrugged and said nothing. After they reached shore and completed the short walk to the cabin, Iacola went in without a backward glance. Davis turned his back to the cabin's entrance, spent several seconds staring at the incredible vista before him, took off his fisherman's hat, sighed, then entered and closed the door.

After a sumptuous dinner of the fish they kept, lightly sautéed zucchini, and pilaf accompanied by one bottle plus of Wild Horse Chardonnay, Iacola surprised Wilson by saying "Have you had second thoughts about playing the game?"

"Yes, I have, for a long time. I just wasn't strong enough to change. I conned myself into thinking the goodies my family and I enjoyed were worth doing something I wasn't proud of. Now my only recourse is philanthropy."

"When I think about the people you'll be joining on that list I figure what the hell, it's a good thing to have all those museums and memorials having to do with culture. I really hope that kind of stuff is a plus for the people. It certainly doesn't put much of a bruise on the givers. Those people have the best tax lawyers available.

"Have you ever looked in that direction, Lee?"

"Sure, but I haven't done much. I've followed the path of least resistance and just blew a lot of smoke."

"What's your idea of blowing smoke?"

"That's another way of saying I wasn't exactly truthful. Now, I'll have to blow a little more smoke and give you a lame excuse…ok here it is. Somehow I got into a conversation with a professor of philosophy. Along with a bunch of other stuff, he told me our country was a place where perception has become reality. Here's how he explained it. People have found how easy it is to give someone an impression that's not true. For example, they can say they have an important position in a company when they're actually a few steps above a janitor. The person receiving this baloney accepts it because they're going to offer more baloney and they want it accepted. I can tell you there's an awful lot of people playing that game, cause I played it a lot and never had a problem and I know for an absolute fact a whole lot of folks laid stuff on me that wasn't true. But, no one gets home free. I knew the negatives caused by my actions. So, I drank more than I would have otherwise and my stress factor was, and probably is, higher than it could be. On a totally different subject, have you ever heard that the air in Alaska can give you a loose mouth? That's the longest speech I've ever made to a friend…and it wasn't the wine."

"I value your friendship, Lee, and it's always nice to become aware of a new, good part of someone you care about. "How do you see this perception is reality thing?"

"About the same as you. I'm particularly aware of the way men practice it on women in the business world. What's surprising is the way they seem to buy into what we're doing. I've believed in women's intuition for a long time. That means most of them can read most of us like a book. A very simple book. I've never come up with an answer why they let us get away with our little games. Any ideas?

"Not really, but I do know one of the reasons we play those games."

"Enlighten me."

"Simple. Our acting like we really know what we're doing is based on the fact that we know, down not so deep, if we gave them the opportunity, an awful lot of them would clean our clocks. Hell, when you think about it, we're not really fair with MEN that we view as a threat to our positions."

"Lee, I've just had a refresher course in something I thought I knew a long time ago."

"And that is?"

"Never judge a book by its cover."

"If that's a compliment, great way to end an evening. Sleep well, my friend."

"Same. Good night."

CHAPTER 8

Some forty-eight hours after their initial meeting Patricia received an evening phone call from Sam.

"You've really got my attention on this thing. I'd like to ask a few questions to be sure I understand the whole concept."

Patricia swallowed hard, hoped her heart wouldn't burst through her chest, then said, "You mean right now?"

Sam hadn't planned it that way but with Patricia's response he realized it would be to his advantage to communicate by phone instead of in person. He wouldn't have to deal with the constant distraction of Patricia's presence. So, "If it's convenient."

"It is."

"Taking care of all the requirements to run as an independent, like getting on the ballot in every state is a monumental challenge. Can it be done?"

"I've already taken care of it. People can vote for the Freedom Party, I hope you like the name, in all fifty. I've also taken all of the necessary steps to protect the name."

"I like Freedom Party. How about the required nationwide campaign machinery?"

"We won't have any. Our appeal for acceptance through TV, radio, print, and the internet will be to all the people of America. Our commitment to them will be to do what we can to improve their lives and the lives of those who come after them. What we say to the people of California will apply to the people of New Hampshire. There won't be different messages for different sections of the country."

Sam was delighted with his decision to communicate by phone. The simplicity of Patricia's concepts were enough of a challenge without his having to continue looking at the space between her eyes.

"What about initial financing to get this thing off the ground?"

"I believe I can generate a large enough media response initially to minimize start up capital requirements. In any event, I'm prepared to provide personal funds as required up to ten million in the form of a loan."

Patricia thought she heard Sam gasp. At any rate there was a pause, then, "I'm not sure you can legally do that. If I'm not mistaken, only the candidate can provide personal funds. I might have something to offer on the subject."

Sam continued, "How would our positions on all the issues be determined?"

"Through discussions between you and I, with you having the final say."

"Aren't you placing a great deal of faith in our degree of compatibility regarding the issues of our time?"

"Yes, but it's well-placed. The same reasons that are the basis for my approaching you in the first place explain why. Additionally, my vibes, intuition and whatever else couldn't be more positive. At the risk of sounding presumptuous, when I'm this sure I'm just never wrong. By the way, you have one other big plus that went right past me. You've been a strong congressional critic regarding ethics, salaries and campaign financing. The knowledge you've gained will help us."

"Should we gather a group of advisers to assist in forming our positions?"

"I don't think so, for two reasons: Number one, advisers offer their counsel with regard to political positions. As you know, we aren't practicing politics. Number two, I have enough faith in our abilities that I believe the two of us will do just fine. All positions are easy to define if you have intellectual integrity and use common sense."

Once again Sam was struck by Patricia's overpowering simplicity. "I'll call you tomorrow morning with my decision."

"Terrific. Look forward to hearing from you."

As Patricia hung up the phone, she was somewhat surprised at her lack of exhilaration now that she felt there was a decent chance that Sam would join her. She decided her mind was so busy with what had to be done she didn't have the mindset to give a great deal of time and energy to Sam's yes or no.

Sam had already decided he would join Patricia. He delayed telling her until the next morning because it was his custom, whenever possible, to see how a decision looked the morning after it had been made.

CHAPTER 9

Now that she had her candidate, Patricia's priorities were clear, a visit to Wyoming for what almost certainly would be a memorable confrontation with her father and finalizing the specifics she'd be discussing with Sam on her return. She could make a good start on the latter on the airplane. When she thought of her first priority she wondered if their meeting would be the beginning of a definitive, negative change in their relationship.

Looking out the aircraft window, Patricia, for the first time focused on what she had been dreading from the instant Sam agreed to become a candidate, the anticipated reaction of her father. It was the height of irony, his triggering the thought processes bringing about the concept of her plan. The specifics of this plan and her participation would go against everything he had always represented and he would be the subject of terrible ridicule from his peers. Coming to grips with her father's hypocrisy would be of some help in weathering the expected explosion from him. She had been aware of this hypocrisy for some time but her desire to think well of her father in a total sense caused her to ignore it. It became increasingly difficult to overlook once she began to spend long periods of time away from him. Looking at a situation from a distance usually allows more objectivity. This is particularly true if the situation includes a charming, much loved, persuasive father.

On the one hand, her father had virtually no respect for his fellow males. Important members of government, business and education along with the legal and medical professions were continuing targets for his criticism. On the other hand, he had played 'The Game' as well as anyone. 'The Game' consisted of winning and never mind the means. Get as much as you can anyway you can and the only no-no is not to get caught. Then you're shunned, not only by the general public but by the other players as well. While Patricia knew her father believed his criticisms (She felt they were accurate), it was also her belief that they were a way to vent his anger at the state of the world and the fact that he wasn't strong enough to go against the tide.

Shortly after arriving at the ranch, Patricia suggested they go into the study for a serious talk. She wanted to get it over with as soon as possible. Within three minutes of their being seated, Patricia told her father what she had done, and then awaited his reaction.

"For God's sake Patricia, do you really understand the ramifications of what you've just said?"

"I believe I do. Relationships, most of them of little importance to me will end or at minimum cool considerably. If we start to gain success, a lot of cheap shots taken by those who want or need for us to fail. Tremendous pressures exerted by members of the Republican Party who will be embarrassed by my actions. More specifically, there will be a zillion rumors and innuendoes regarding the nature of my relationship with Sam. Not to mention a work schedule over an extended period of time that will make previous efforts seem like child's play. Does that about cover it?"

"Almost, but you left out the most important negative, your personal safety. It just may be that I have a better understanding of your undertaking than either you or Sam. Should lightning strike so that real success is a possibility, there are people in this country, I guarantee you, who wouldn't hesitate a minute to do whatever it takes to stop you. That includes termination of the breathing process."

Patricia had been so prepared to do battle with her father on different grounds; she was caught off guard by his response. She had never experienced such intensity from him. She was about to ask him if his concern for her safety was primary when he surprised her again.

"If you're thinking I'm being overly dramatic or that I'm telling you this as a smoke screen, you're wrong on both counts. If I understand your premise correctly, some very powerful people will view you and Sam as serious threats, not only to their personal interests but to the welfare of this country. When people such as these get excited, the life of one or two individuals, even people such as you and Sam, become unimportant. As to my remark about a smoke screen, hell yes, I'd rather not go through all the stuff I'll be taking from my peers about my crazy daughter. But that's a minor inconvenience because I'm so very proud of what you're going to try. With all my business successes, you and I both know I'm a hypocrite. On the one hand, I rail against the lack of integrity throughout our society, particularly in business. On the other hand, I'm no better than they are, at least in my business dealings. I've watched you very carefully since you've

36

been in Washington. I know you've tried to fit in with those jerks. If anything, I'm envious that you have the guts and the opportunity to try and break out of that mess and take a shot, a very long shot, at changing the status quo. Also, one hypocrite in the Reinhardt family is way too much."

Patricia was dumbfounded. After all the years, how could she have missed this dimension of her father? She walked towards him, her eyes filling with tears, put her arms around his neck, hugged him tightly and said, "Thank you."

"Thank you. I feel very fortunate to be your father. In all of this crazy, ridiculous world you're the one constant that has always enriched my life. I'm just being selfish in trying to make certain that nothing happens to you. I really do wish you every success and if you start to achieve any, I reserve the right to take whatever steps I believe necessary to protect you. I know a guy in Israel who takes care of such matters. Would you allow your foolish, proud father such an indulgence?"

"Promise."

CHAPTER 10

Shortly after her return from Wyoming, Patricia met with Sam.

"Have you got the specifics on ending your effort as the American consumer's number one friend?"

"It'll take fifteen days to turn all of my current projects over to my associates. Somehow that doesn't seem very long to wind up a lifetime's work but then I've been fortunate to be surrounded by a number of bright, energetic, highly motivated people. Besides, we don't often complete a project. The best we can do is make progress. For example, take Detroit. When can you say that cars and trucks offer maximum protection from injury, have minimal impact on our environment and are as economical as possible to operate?"

"I understand. O. K. Samuel, here we go. Number one, we have to form our positions on all the issues we'll be putting forth." Then, half jokingly, "Shall we do that right now?"

"Let's give it a try."

Incredibly, after an intense two hours, so efficient that hardly a minute was wasted, they had their positions on what they considered the important issues:

ECONOMY: We will make every effort to bring about a reduction in the cost and size of the Federal Government while giving the highest priority to maximizing government revenues by providing a favorable climate for American business. The findings of the committee headed by Mr. Bowles and Mr. Simpson will have a major influence on this effort. We anticipate that the cumulative effect from these areas of emphasis will cause a decrease in the unemployment rate.

FOREIGN POLICY: Economics should be the cornerstone of U.S. foreign policy. If we're not strong economically in a global sense, we're not a real super power. While the military will continue to be an integral part of foreign policy, we must have an ever increasing emphasis on relationships designed to advance American economic interests. As far as political and/or military strife are concerned, we should contribute to their solutions in direct proportion to all other major countries of the western world.

A strong, long range energy policy should be the most important factor regarding our foreign policy in the Middle East. It's sheer insanity that we're dependent on foreign oil some 39 years after the disruption of the early seventies. America continues as the place where our city lights burn brightly through the night and large gas guzzling vehicles of all types clog our nations highways. In order to sustain this lunacy we spend the lives of the individuals making up the one segment of our society for which everyone should have the highest respect, the magnificent men and women of our armed services. We will work diligently and with a strong sense of purpose for the day when a substantial American presence is no longer necessary in this unstable, dangerous part of the world.

HEALTH CARE: Our first priority will be health insurance for the fifty million Americans without it. Our second priority will be to reduce fraud and other misdeeds from providers of medical services for Medicare and Medicaid. We will also review the business practices of insurance companies that provide services to the US Government.

EDUCATION: Ms. Reinhardt's number one priority will be leading a national attempt to improve the quality of the K through 12 educational process in America. Accordingly, I will not appoint a Secretary of Education. In all instances, she will have available all the resources of the Executive branch of our government. More specifically she will be addressing, in order of their importance, the quality and income of our teachers, class size, the upgrading of current educational facilities and a lengthening of the school day and school year.

While I am aware of the limited role the Federal government should play in American education, I feel there is a need to bring about a common national approach to many of education's problems. Such an approach would help insure a quality factor that would apply to all American students.

"O.K., so much for the Saviur manifesto. Now let's set a place and date for the announcement of your candidacy. It's my suggestion we hold it at a prominent hotel here in Washington. What do you think?"

"Makes sense logically. Most of the major news people are here. How are you going to get the info to the media?"

"Notices to the political publications on the internet plus major networks plus NY Times, Washington Post, Time Magazine, Newsweek, etc?"

"What can we expect regarding attendance?"

"Depends on what's breaking news-wise in the time frame we set. If we have some kind of catastrophe or a really big happening on the national or international political scene, we've got a problem."

"One thing for sure, your last press conference won't hurt."

Patricia's eyes almost danced as she said, "I hope that's the case, although I was just saying what I really thought, just as we'll be doing."

Sam wondered if he'd ever be able to look Patricia in the eye without short circuiting at least part of his mental capabilities. Just when he thought the worst was over, he'd regress and have to redouble his efforts, but he was making progress.

From Patricia, "How about May 15th?"

"Sounds OK to me. Now that we've got our positions and the time and place for our declaration, question: How are we going to represent our effort to the American people? We don't want to sound sanctimonious and we certainly don't want to proclaim our virtues. Remember Jimmy Barter's 'I'll never lie to you'?"

"Once again, Samuel, simplicity. We'll tell the media and American people that we won't practice the politics of today. We'll also tell them we're well awre of the broken promises in today's world. So, let our actions determine whether we're for real. I haven't mentioned this yet but I suggest that ten dollars be the maximum amount we will accept from any one source, individual, corporate, whatever. That will certainly be a departure from 2012 politics."

"With that limit, shouldn't you be concerned about getting your loan back?"

"I don't think so. If I was thinking in terms of the American voter of the last four or five Presidential elections, that would be a different story. I'm suggesting that we bet the farm on the more than eighty million eligible voters that have dropped out., that are never heard from. If I'm right, within thirty days of the press conference and the announcement of our positions we'll know our chances. The number of ten dollar contributions will be the answer."

"When will we announce our positions?"

"At the press conference, but you won't take questions. You will promise to explain all of them in detail."

"Since you're on such a roll, give me your vision of this campaign."

"The use of television, radio, the print media and the internet. Initially, you'll respond to questions from the public and various panels regarding our positions on national TV and radio programs. From national we'll go to every state and appear on the same type of programs. Additionally, we will publish our positions and take questions on our website. If public acceptance is strong enough, we can consider, late in the campaign, public appearances at a few educational facilities."

"Aren't we talking major, major bucks here?"

"It won't be cheap but I believe we'll end up spending a lot less than recent presidential candidates."

"I understand now what you meant when you said I wouldn't have to participate in conventional campaign activities. This is more of a cerebral theme."

"Right on. Our approach will be to logic and reason. However, on your TV and radio appearances you should invite questions of a personal nature. Whatever they want to know about your early years, family, why you became a consumer advocate, etc. It's important they come to know you."

On the few occasions when Sam's emotions rose to a high level, his physical reaction was to feel a tingling sensation in the area of his spine. This time the tingling seemed to race over his entire body. "Magnificent, magnificent simplicity."

"I'm glad you approve. Otherwise we'd have our first disagreement."

"OK, enough specifics for today. How'd it go with your father?"

Patricia, while surprised that he knew of her trip to Wyoming, didn't hesitate and said, "Much better than I expected. Thanks for asking."

Patricia moved to within a foot of where Sam was standing, extended her hand and while looking directly into his eyes said, "I don't know what lies ahead for us Sam since I have no frame of reference. I can only tell you I'll try my best to justify your faith in me."

"I can't ask for more but please don't worry about any responsibility you believe you have for my joining you. I'm certainly at a point in life where I can accept complete responsibility for my actions. If anything, I'm beholden to you for bringing an exciting new dimension to my life. The more I think about it the more pumped I get. Call you soon." With that, Sam ambled out the door.

As soon as Sam left, Patricia called her secretary into her office. She first swore her to secrecy, then explained in detail her future plans. Patricia asked if she would like to continue in her position. The two women had developed strong, mutual respect and trust in each other and Elizabeth, without hesitation, said she would be happy to stay on.

CHAPTER 11

The 15th of May proved to be a great choice for holding the press conference announcing Sam's candidacy. Nationally there were no happenings of import regarding activities of the government or financial communities. Additionally, there were no disasters of any type worldwide outside of a terrible train wreck in India.

The attendance exceeded Patricia's expectations. Not only were all of the important media entities there but most were represented by their heavy hitters: Arianna Huffington of the Huffington Post, Rachel Maddow of MSNBC, Brian Williams of NBC, and Frank Rich of the New York Times.

While the strong attendance, for the most part, was caused by the quiet news front, there was considerable interest generated by the unusual, if not strange combination of Patricia, the now former Republican Senator from a conservative background and Sam, consumer activist and adversary of corporate America. It should also be said that Patricia's presence was a positive in terms of attendance by male media representatives.

The press conference was held in the Camelia Room of the Washington Hilton. At exactly 3:00 P.M., Patricia and Sam stepped from behind a blue floor to ceiling curtain and walked directly to the center of the stage where the banks of microphones were located.

Both stood there for a moment trying not to blink too much in the glare of floodlights. Sam then went before the microphones and said, "Thank you for coming." A pause, then, "I hereby announce my candidacy for President of the United States. I'll be running as an Independent. Senator Reinhardt will be our candidate for Vice President. We will answer questions for fifteen minutes then I will put forth my positions on what I consider today's major issues facing America."

A moment of stunned silence, considerable murmuring, then from Rachel Maddow, "Mr. Saviur....haven't you already indicated your candidacy for this year's election?

From Sam with a warm smile: "Ms. Maddow, don't you ever miss anything? Yes, I did declare and you must be one of three people in the whole country aware of my action. I'm sure 2012 would have turned out the same as the other times. However from what Ms. Reinhardt has conveyed to me I have a strong feeling this year will be a lot different. Now I'll go out on a limb and anticipate your follow up. Here's why: After a lifetime of trying to be a positive force affecting the lives of the people of America I've decided to try to hasten the process."

Maddow again, "Would you elaborate?"

"As you might imagine, operating as a consumer advocate through the judicial system, the political system and various methods of education is a very slow process. I'm certain I can pick up the pace from the office of President as well as expanding the areas I can impact."

From Arianna Huffington, "Aren't you susceptible to the same knock put on others over the years, that before running for President you should run for, win and successfully perform in elective office?"

"I'm obviously susceptible but I consider my not having participated in politics a big plus. I am beholden to no one, including financial backers or political cronies. Additionally, I have no experience in the pathetic process of what passes for political campaigns today. I have an absolutely clean slate to write on. In simple terms, I am not a politician and that may be a plus in terms of voter acceptance. As a matter of fact, this is a good place to establish the cornerstone of our effort: Senator Reinhardt and I today pledge to the American people that we will do everything in our power NOT to practice politics in our pursuit of the Presidency. Contrary to what many believe we don't think there's anything wrong with the governmental system set up by the founders of this country. We believe the problem lies with the people who populate this system and the activities of these individuals. To us, politics circa 2012 is the sum of these activities.

Today, politics means caving in or pandering to special interests who are major financial contributors. Taking credit for positives and blaming the opposition for negatives; Giving personal goals such as re-election or moving to a higher office a higher priority than the best interests of the American people; Adopting an 'any means justifies the end' mentality. We will not participate in such disgraceful behavior. We will define America's challenges with intellectual integrity and propose solutions based on logic and reason without trying to please any particular group. We will only be beholden to the people of America, all of them.

It's important to me that you understand how this cornerstone originated. While it has always been my nature to be a-political, it was the Senator who enunciated our policy of no politics. She did so based on her observations and participation in our political system."

A hint of a smile from Patricia, then Mary Thomas of United News, "Mr. Saviur, would you please enlighten us on the relationship...let me rephrase that. Isn't the alliance between you and Senator Reinhardt to be considered as surprising and somewhat unusual?"

Sam smiled and said, "Since she bears the primary responsibility for our standing before you today, she, better than I, can respond to your questions."

Patricia, who was standing a few steps behind and to the right of Sam moved forward to a point right next to him. Sam hesitated for a few seconds then stepped to his left.

"I've been concerned for some time now about the appalling lack of leadership on a national level. I don't see any changes taking place in the foreseeable future and the problems facing our country at home and abroad continue to increase in severity. A little over a month ago I decided to act and called Mr. Saviur."

From John Jones of Rolling Stone, "With all of the presidential aspirants in evidence, many with political organizations already in place, why Mr. Saviur?"

"Because of what I perceive to be his integrity, strength of character and lifelong dedication to the best interests of the American people. To anticipate what might be your next question, no, I don't know anyone else who can match Mr. Saviur in those areas. Once again, that's my personal opinion."

From Frank Rich of the New York Times, "Two part question: What will be your specific role in Mr.

Saviur's campaign? Also, as you know, the costs of political campaigns today are astronomical. Can you raise enough money?"

"I will be Mr. Saviur's campaign manager. As to finances, we will try to raise sufficient funds by going directly to the American people."

Rich again, "Would you go into more detail about going directly to the voting public for money?"

"In the interests of maintaining our timetable, I won't discuss the mechanics of our fund raising but I will tell you that the maximum contribution we will accept from any one source is ten dollars."

Silence, a few snickers, then a clamor for recognition. Patricia quickly pointed to the syndicated columnist Richard Cohen of the Washington Post. She had long admired his objective and fair reporting. "Senator Reinhardt, in this age of PAC's and special interests isn't your approach somewhat naïve?"

"Perhaps, perhaps. I'm not speaking for Mr. Saviur now but it's my personal opinion that we have to get that part of the American electorate, that vast silent group we never or seldom hear from, really interested in our campaign. If we're successful in doing this our approach may not be naïve. If we're not successful then we won't be needing a great deal of money."

Brian Williams of NBC: "Senator Reinhardt, would you mind sharing your father's reaction to this remarkable change in your political career?"

Patricia smiled warmly and said, "Yes, I would mind, but I will tell you that my father has always had my respect and my love. As I stand here, nothing has happened to change those feelings. I'm sorry but that will be the last question I'll take. After all, Mr. Saviur is the candidate."

With that she stepped away from the microphone as Sam came forward and said "Prior to the election I will announce our complete team which will include all cabinet members. Doing this might seem a bit presumptuous since our effort must be successful for these positions to take effect. We feel, however, that the American voter should know as much as possible as soon as possible. Now, here are my positions on important issues facing America in 2012.

After Sam completed his reading there was a strong clamoring for recognition. The noise level rose to a point where Sam gestured for silence which he never received. The continuing commotion was reduced enough, however, for him to say, "Finally, in recent weeks I've heard many of the candidates for President begin one of their 'promises' with an 'I will.....'. They don't seem to understand. A President needs the approval of Congress on most of their endeavors. There is some room for action in a President's position as commander in chief of the US Military. Accordingly, if elected, I will begin the process of bringing our troops in Afghanistan home. This action will begin within thirty days of my inauguration. I know we're ending on a provocative note but we have nothing more to say at this time and I'd rather stop than stand here and not answer your questions directly. I've never practiced that sort of response and I don't intend to start now. Once again, thank you so much for coming and I look forward to seeing you soon."

Sam and Patricia stood together, smiled and waved for a moment then moved behind the curtain located to the rear of the podium.

The instant they were alone Patricia clasped both of Sam's hands in hers and said, "That was a stupendous, surprising ending; we've never discussed troop withdrawal from Afghanistan. You may not care for it, Samuel, but based on what I just saw and heard, you have the stuff to be one hell of a player."

"Bite your tongue. Player means politics."

"Whoops, you're right."

"I'm sorry I didn't mention the Afghanistan statement. It's an area I feel very strongly about. I hope you don't mind. It won't happen again."

"No problem, we're completely in sync."

While he was elated by Patricia's remarks, Sam wondered how long it would take to feel really comfortable around this creature. The combination of her happy, animated face and close proximity along with the effect of her holding both of his hands caused a momentary expression, almost of pain. Patricia was too excited to pick up on it. After what Sam thought was an inordinate delay in responding to Patricia's outburst he said, "My final remarks weren't based on what I thought would play well, I just expressed my feelings."

Not letting go of his hands, Patricia said, "That's the beauty of it. As I said early on, you don't have to do or say anything you don't believe or don't want to say. Being yourself is going to be a refreshing and I think appealing change from what the people of this country have been used to hearing. Whatever happens, let's remain constant to that premise. Gotta run. Now that the world knows, I have to get started on the thousand and one things on my agenda. Call you soon." With that she was gone, leaving Sam to figure how to leave the building without seeing any media reps.

CHAPTER 12

Ted Burner watched Patricia and Sam's news conference from his New York City apartment. As soon as it was over he immediately switched to CNN and was disappointed to see continuing coverage of a murder trial. Even though it had been many years since his participation in the management of CNN, its downward spiral bothered him, a lot. After all, he was its' originator.

While Patricia was the main reason for his thought processes switching back to the news conference, he had always respected Sam. The straightforward, unique approach he and Patricia were taking rang a lot of Ted's bells. Their clanging reached a level that brought about a connection between his impression of the news conference and the current condition of CNN.

In an earlier timeframe Burner had identified the primary problems facing the world while doing his part to help solve them. Since then he had severed his business relationships and there had been some deterioration in his physical condition. He was tuned in to what was happening in his beloved country, much of it indicating very serious, near term problems. Why not change direction and become involved in the 2012 election for President?

As a rule, the time between one of Ted's ideas and taking action could be measured in seconds. True to form, he picked up the phone. Some thirty minutes later he had received a green light on becoming the head of all programming for CNN. That meant he would determine all content 24 hours a day, seven days a week through the 31st of December, 2012. His total earnings would be determined within one week of that date. Five million dollars plus expenses was guaranteed. All other monies received would be based on CNN's ratings at the time of his leaving. The deal would be finalized within 72 hours by Ted signing a simple contract. Another result of his phone call was the number of Patricia's private line.

Patricia had been in her office for ten minutes after returning from the press conference when she was told that Ted Burner was calling. "What can I do for you Mr. Burner?"

"I'm calling you 'stead of Sam because it's my impression you're behind this whole thing. Besides, you're a hell of a lot prettier than he is. I'd like to meet with you as soon as possible and decide how interested I should be in what you folks are up to."

Patricia glanced at her watch and calculated that it had been no more than thirty five minutes since the end of the press conference. Marveling at the speed of Burner's response, she hesitated a few seconds too long.

"Hello, hello."

"We haven't been disconnected, Mr. Burner. I'd be delighted to meet with you. Where and when?"

"Duke Zeibert's at 1:00 tomorrow. If it's convenient, have a cab drop you at the side entrance. There will be an attendant waiting there to escort you to a private dining room."

"No problem, look forward…"

As she put down the phone, Patricia realized Burner hadn't said goodbye. This is too much, she thought. We're going to bet the farm on TV and I get a call from a guy who was one of the heaviest hitters in the business, within an hour of the announcement. As she marveled at her good fortune she didn't have the slightest clue that had she been any other person on the Washington scene she would not have heard from CNN's former owner. That the biological occurrence resulting in her stunning appearance was really the factor that tipped the scales in favor of Burner making the call. So much for the substantial number of Americans who figure there are deep, complicated reasoning processes involved in major political happenings.

CHAPTER 13

Within fifteen minutes after watching Sam's announcement, James Barville called the President. A rather surprised chief executive took the call just as he was about to begin dinner.

"Mr. President, I would assume you know that Sam Saviur's declared his candidacy for President?"

"Yes, someone mentioned it in passing this afternoon but I didn't give it much attention. Should I?"

"I want to be the first to go on record as saying that this guy could give us a great deal of trouble."

"Seems to me he's going to be climbing an awful steep hill with a big rock on his back. He's got to form a national organization and raise an awful lot of money starting from ground zero, all in a very short time frame."

"I hear you and you're right on but my stomach never fails me and right now it's acting up something fierce. This guy is one tough dude. More than that, I don't see him leaving his lifelong crusade unless he's got an awful good game plan. Most worrisome of all is his teaming with former Senator Reinhardt."

"THAT is tough to figure. Why is she of such concern to you?"

"Having known her father for many years, I've been able to gain a little insight regarding the Senator. I want to tell you she just might be the kind of individual who could drive us crazy and I'm not being facetious. One thing I'll tell you right now, 2008 is going to look like a walk in the park compared to what we're dealing with in 2012. Sorry to burden you with these negatives so quickly after the announcement, Mr. President, but you know me. I like to jump right on things."

"No problem. Appreciate your concern. Take a little Maalox and talk to you soon."

"Good evening, Mr. President."

As soon as he hung up, Barville thought, you know your instincts are right and this guy and this woman are going to give us fits.

You also know you're like a little boy buttering up his teacher to call the President so quickly. Looks like some interesting times ahead but for right now, might as well give John a call.

John DeSantis had served on the police force in Washington for twenty five years, the last eight as chief. Since his retirement at age fifty-five, he had been a very selective detective. If John didn't have first hand knowledge, he had several sources he could tap regarding the important people on the Washington scene. He sold this information for a steep price. This income plus a substantial pension allowed him to live comfortably in a Georgetown condominium. He had been retained by Barville on three occasions over the years but hadn't talked to him for some time.

"Been a while Jim, what's up?"

"Should I hire you to tell me about Sam Saviur?"

"Since you've been a good client and because this will take no more than three minutes, I'll chalk up what I'm about to say to P.R. and I know you won't forget my generosity. This guy doesn't own a car, he's lived in the same efficiency apartment since he's been in Washington and I doubt that any of his clothes are les than fifteen years old. All his food consumption takes place in different beaneries around town. He's never eaten a meal that's taken longer than five minutes from the time he walks in the door. Except for an occasional movie, his entire life is his work. Some of the slickest operators in this country have looked him over and as you know a few of the top boys have tried to set him up. Complete waste of time. This guy's so clean he'd give Mother Theresa a complex. Did that take three minutes?"

"Not quite John and I do appreciate your help. Still drinking that single malt scotch?"

"Yeah, never found anything better."

John heard a 'Good night;' then a click. He smiled, secure in the knowledge he'd be receiving a case of McAllams in the near future.

While Barville hadn't expected other than what he'd heard from John, he still felt disappointment. Oh well, there was always the Senator to work over. He smiled ruefully at the realization there was very little context in which he could think of her without some application of Freudian comment.

CHAPTER 14

When she arrived at the restaurant, Patricia was immediately ushered into the dining room reserved for VIP's. Burner ended his phone conversation upon seeing Patricia.

"Hope you approve of my choice of restaurants. In the old days I came here once or twice a month as a favor to Larry Queen. He and Duke are long time friends."

"As far as important meetings are concerned, food doesn't mean much. I've never learned to eat and talk at the same time. Tea is usually it."

"I hear you. What drives me nuts is the ordering process. I get the impression a lot of people put more thought into what they're going to eat than the reason for the meeting."

Burner pushed a button next to his napkin. A waiter appeared within seconds, took the order for tea and a bowl of soup then quickly disappeared.

From Burner: "Since we live in a country where perception has become reality, I got that line from Larry, I wanted to find out where you're coming from. There are only two possibilities: You're the best I've seen in creating a perception or you're the real thing. I'll have the answer when we leave here."

"Why do you want to know where I'm coming from?"

"Good question. As soon as your press conference ended I set up a deal where I have 72 hours to decide whether I want to accept the position of CNN's head of programming. I know what Sam can do. I don't have a clue about you. If you're the real thing I'll accept the job and be a major factor in getting out your campaign's message."

"Wouldn't you run into trouble in terms of favoring a particular party?"

"The way CNN is going they're not in a position to raise hell. Besides, after watching the parade of clowns in the recent primary, and I cleaned that up, we're in an age where anything goes. Finally, if you and Sam amaze everyone by winning, CNN would look pretty good to a lot of people who are not tuning in right now."

"At this stage of your life, why are you doing this?"

"This 'stage' is a primary reason. As a final surprising action to remember T.B., I'd like to play an important role in a project that could help this magnificent country. Besides, I've led a pretty dull existence in recent times. What you folks are trying to do should liven things up a little."

"I hope what you say is true. If it is, you'll be the first business 'tycoon' I've ever met who doesn't place his personal success and/or his company's success above everything."

Burner couldn't believe what he'd heard. NO ONE ever expressed doubt about anything he said. Without any indication of his surprise he said, "Can't say I blame you for feeling that way." Then, smiling, "I've seen a little of that over the years. I'm not making any proclamations about my character, but it's as simple as this: I've learned there needn't be conflict with the priorities just given you. In fact, they can be so compatible as to help me reach my ultimate goals and still look at myself in the mirror without cringing, but that's a story for another day. Now, would you please tell me the motivation behind this whole thing?"

"Forgive me for sounding impertinent Mr. Burner. Unless you believe I'm playing some kind of game, you must know my motivation. In a way that will insure a bright future for this country, I want to be a positive force in the life of every American.

Once again, Burner was startled. First the surprise that he would be questioned on anything he said, then a lesson in direct, powerful conversation, something he considered a Burner trademark. In an instant he realized that Patricia was in a different league when compared to just about everyone he had dealt with in recent memory. He would have to switch to another gear quickly.

"I was hoping that would be your answer but I guess I wanted to hear you say it. Would you mind giving me some specifics regarding your plans to improve education in America?"

Patricia was surprised that Burner would ask her about education rather than business. "Any particular reason why you want our views on that subject?"

"I share your belief that this is the biggest challenge and/or need we face in the coming years."

"Fair enough. As Sam has indicated, the primary areas that must be addressed are: The quality of teachers, the upgrading of facilities, the number of students per class and a lengthening of the school day and the school year. The last two don't need much explanation so I'll concentrate on teacher quality plus one other concept that Sam didn't mention. I want to warn you, this will take a while."

"No problem."

"OK here we go. Before going any further, when I refer to young people and education I mean students in kindergarten through high school. In the history of the world, there has never been a nation where young people have been as entertained as those in America. Even youngsters on the lower end of the economic scale have access, at minimum, to TV. I won't even go into the effects of the methods of communication.

In order for teachers to reach the students of today, you could say they're competing with this entertainment. A teacher must be exceptional in his or her ability to communicate in a way that will cause the students to listen. They need high verbal skills along with enthusiasm and a sense of humor. They must have a high sensitivity factor and a strong sense of self so they can anticipate and then cope with the challenges they'll face on a daily basis. They should also have some clue of what's going on in the minds of the students. Finally, the students must feel their teachers care about them as individuals.

It goes without saying that knowing subject matter backwards and forwards is primary but doesn't count for much if you can't get and maintain the student's attention. I realize I'm asking a lot and I have no illusions about how difficult it will be to reach this level, but I know that most students will accept and respond positively to the qualities I've just described. I also know that individuals possessing these qualities are out there. We just have to get them into our classrooms."

"Question. You said 'most students'. What about those that don't respond? What about the problem student that engages in disruptive behavior?"

"After determining that the problem is not the result of a learning or personality disability, all possible would be done to correct the problem. If the results are negative, the student is out of there.

I know that's hard nosed, but you can't sacrifice the best interests of the decent students for one or two troublemakers. Of course we would try to create a learning environment for problem students."

"Even though you've described a super teacher and you say that the young people of today will respond to such teachers, do you have any examples of substance?"

"I've kept it pretty quiet and I'm not saying I'm a super teacher, but I taught a class in a very poor section of a small town in Wyoming. It was pretty rough in the beginning but by the time I left, we had accomplished our academic objectives and were getting along quite well. I'm also not saying that one example makes my case, but there's no doubt in my mind that the qualities I've mentioned are necessary for success."

"In the sixteen plus years I spent in school I don't need one hand to count the teachers that came close to your version of what we need."

"My educational experience in that regard is identical to yours. I'm sure you share my thoughts, however, in realizing how much the ones we can count contributed to our learning process as well as our outlook on life. We just have to do our best to attract and develop people that have those capabilities."

"I would imagine you just might have something to offer on that subject."

Patricia smiled mischievously and said, "I'm surprised you would say that. However, I'll give it a try.

Number one, it wouldn't be easy to become a teacher. Initially, applicants would be tested for personality traits, communication skills, sensitivity level, etc. Once accepted they would engage in regular undergraduate work while they continued working on their communication skills as well as actually teaching. Most of their fifth year would be spent teaching. In all cases, the opinions of the students they teach would be the single most important evaluating factor. As far as I'm concerned, developing the ability to teach should be emphasized above knowledge of subject matter. That area is a given and is easily tested.

I've over simplified but I think you get the picture."

"I certainly do. Now, how are you going to attract people of this quality?"

"In a word, money. Do you know how many individuals I've talked to in American business, who, by their own evaluations, are working at twenty five percent of realistic capacity and being paid twice what elementary and secondary teachers are making? This statement refers to people who are at comparable stages of their careers. To make matters even more ridiculous, the twenty five percent figure by no stretch means these efforts are much more than mediocre. It's absolute insanity that we expect people in the public sector to be God-like with regard to the characteristics of their vocational efforts. To me, one of the most terrible indictments of our society's values is the fact that teachers have had to organize into unions in their attempts to be treated fairly.

"What I'm saying applies to other public sectors of our society as well. Some years ago, Ronald Reagan, in his infinite wisdom, broke the Air Traffic Controllers Union. These people made a lot less than pilots and are doing well if they're not near "burnout" by the time their in their forties. The rationale you hear most frequently as to why pilots are higher paid is their responsibility for the safety of the people they're transporting. By those criteria, the controllers are responsible for the safety of more people in one hour than the pilots are for a month of Sundays. Has anyone ever counted the number of passengers riding on planes that are under the guidance of a controller in the tower at O'Hare in Chicago? For just one hour? You tell me. A good teacher with five years experience should be making at least one hundred thousand dollars a year. However, because of the salary level, there would be no tenure. You could only stay if you maintain certain standards. For those who say we can't afford higher salaries for teachers I say we can't afford NOT to pay fair salaries so we can attract the best and brightest. After all, this is a capitalistic society. I also have a few thoughts on how to fund these increased salaries but I'm running short on time.

Finally, I would like to see a top of the line commission examine the pros and cons of dividing students on the basis of gender, starting in the fifth grade. I have what I think are terrific reasons for believing it's a good idea but I'll leave that subject for another day also. Now, aren't you sorry you got me started?"

Burner was so mesmerized he didn't utter a sound for some seconds before putting forth a rather distant "No." Then, after literally shaking his head as if to remove water from his ears, he said "O.K., now let's get to the details of your plan in getting your message to the American people. Before you begin, would you please call me Ted? Formality has never appealed to me."

"Alright, Ted. Obviously, TV will be first, followed by the internet, radio and the print media."

"Even though he's retired, Larry would be the 'go-to' guy for TV. The fact that he likes Sam won't hurt."

"With all due respect, Larry may have lost a step or two, but I'll be happy to talk to him if he's interested."

Burner was feeling comfortable again. Her comment on Larry Queen didn't phase him.

"Good. In terms of time, how long and how often?"

"Enough programs to cover all of the issues we consider important along with ongoing thirty second commercials delivered by Sam and I. These commercials would emphasize our positions regarding America's problem areas. We would never mention our opponents."

"Sounds about right. Here's what I'm offering. Number one, you can deal directly with me. You'll never talk to anyone else at CNN except my personal secretary. Number two, my credit terms will be liberal. At ten bucks per contribution it could take a while to develop a strong cash flow. Number three, within limits, I'll help advise you regarding the time and dates of your programs."

"Mr. Burner, pardon me, Ted. Far be it for me to advise you but, again, aren't you leaving yourself open for some heavy criticism regarding objectivity and equal treatment?"

"I've answered part of that question before but in general I couldn't care less. Since the beginning of our meeting this whole thing with you and Sam has come into focus. By recalling what you've said in the past about the wars, our lack of an effective energy policy and remembering the positions put forth at your press conference, these impressions combined with what I've learned from this meeting…I'm convinced I want to join your effort. Its importance goes far beyond that of any commercial venture. And, you know what? If you're right and you folks carry the day, my network will be closely identified with one of the most momentous happenings in political history. That's not too shabby."

Now it was Patricia's turn to be impressed. This man, who in person was smaller and almost frail looking compared to the pictures of him on his yacht, had put down some heavy stuff in a short time frame. "Ted, I couldn't ask for more than you've offered. I'll get back to you within a couple of days. Now, if you'll excuse me, I've got to get on the road. Long ways to go and not much time to get there."

Burner, while disappointed that their meeting was ending so quickly, responded by offering to drop Patricia at her next stop. Patricia accepted.

As they left through the VIP exit to his waiting limo, Burner knew, without question, Patricia was the real thing.

CHAPTER 15

After returning to her office from the meeting with Burner, Patricia immediately called Sam. She told him of Burner's extraordinary offers of his network's services and his counsel. She then indicated their number one priority was to get the transcript of their press conference on their website. Shortly thereafter, on CNN and on their website, they would announce the host, date and time of their first TV program.

On this first program, Sam would extend a standing offer to debate anyone who would agree to a format where there would be no moderator, just the two participants asking questions of each other with no time limit on the answer. His opponent would also agree to practice civility; only one person talking at a time. Finally, since it wasn't likely that there would be any sponsor, his opponent would agree to pay for one-half the cost of the television time.

While Patricia initially had her doubts about him as the CNN host, she finally settled on Larry Queen. She had spent a very intense hour getting a first hand impression of this famous TV personality.

There were two main factors in Patricia's decision: Larry proved to be one of the brightest people she had ever encountered along with the fact that he came across as an unpretentious, flat out nice person.

CHAPTER 16

"Sam, nice seeing you again. You know you're one of the very few who could bring me back into the studio. Of course, Ted Burner threatening me with bodily harm was also a factor. Since I clearly remember the efficiency of our conversations, why are you doing this? It's not the first time you've run for president."

"Nice to see you Larry. My past efforts originated out of frustration with the leadership of our country. I had a strong distaste for the political practices of both parties. I knew I couldn't participate using the same approach. I also didn't realize I had a viable alternative. More on that later. When you add in the media's trashing me as a spoiler, to say I didn't do well was an understatement."

"What's your response to being a "spoiler" in 2012?"

"How can you spoil something that's already going bad so fast you can smell it in Baltimore? I'm referring of course to all three branches of government in Washington D.C."

"Samuel! I'm rarely at a loss for words but I'm pretty close right now. In all the years we've known each other I've never heard you express yourself in that manner."

"Larry, here is the short answer to your accurate comment. In all my years in Washington, I've never witnessed a member of congress saying "You lie" to the President when he's making a major speech. I've never seen a Supreme Court Justice make an ass of himself at another important speech by the President. I've never heard the leader of the senate conservatives say that his number one priority is getting the President out of the White House. This terrible behavior is the response to a chief executive, toward whom I'll offer some constructive criticism shortly, but he has practiced civility. And what has this civility gotten him? Nothing but scorn and ridicule. We're really way past the time when someone needs to tell it like it is. There's been a fair amount of dancing around that area. A well known TV journalist flat out called one of the conservative candidates for President a liar. Based on what I've heard from this guy, the candidate, that term fits nicely."

"Then there's that old question "Do two wrongs make a right?"

"I look at it a little differently. Some of the people I've just mentioned are either bullies or not the brightest bulbs on the Christmas tree or both. That means you have to get their attention. I don't enjoy this approach but it's certainly worth a try."

"You indicated some constructive criticism toward the President?"

"Two main areas. I know hindsight is easy but he should have started pulling our troops out of Iraq and Afghanistan within sixty days of his inauguration. Secondly, he should have been a lot more hardnosed in dealing with the people in the three examples I've mentioned. I won't go into his congressional opposition. Our time limits are too short."

"Give me an example of what you would have done with one of those three people you mentioned."

"If I was President, making a speech and this Supreme Court justice indicated his displeasure with something I'd said I would have stopped talking, addressed him and said that he had two choices. One was to voice his feelings so everyone could hear and I would respond, immediately. If he chose not to be heard I would suggest that he mind his manners."

"WOW is the best I can do."

"You know Larry, there's irony at work here. The first time I heard the words 'In America, perception has become reality', was..?"

"On my program and they came from me."

"What a memory! As we speak millions upon millions of every persuasion are playing that game. An out growth of this craziness? Anyone can say anything and if they say it enough times it becomes fact. A good example? Several conservative members of congress have promised Grover Sorquist that they would not vote for a tax increase. And who is Grover Sorquist? Just a guy who has proclaimed his opposition to any tax increase so often he's become the poster boy for those who agree with him. The media is the main carrier of this nonsense. Somehow we've got to slow it down."

"Remembering my 'perception has become reality' comment plus what you've said about it guarantees I'll be up a little later than my normal bedtime tonite. We'll be taking calls right after the break."

71

"Cynthiana, Kentucky."

"This is for Mr. Saviur. I haven't understood a hell of a lot of what you folks have been sayin' but I would like to hear what you'd do about our country's financial situation."

"There's a list of recommendations that's been out for some time. It was produced by a bi-partisan group and it's called the Bowles-Simpson report. That report would be a major influence on my actions. If you care to read it, I'm sure it's on the internet."

Cynthiana, Ky – "If it's so damn good why haven't I heard more about it?"

"It makes too much sense for the members of congress to stand up and move on it."

"Decatur, Illinois"

"About that odor coming out of Washington, do you think it's coming from a government too big to move? After a while, if you can't move, decay becomes a factor."

"There's always room for reductions but there's nothing wrong with our system of government. The problem lies with the people who make up the system."

"Winnemucca, Nevada."

"I'm a longtime member of the National Rifle Association. You for or against."

"I rarely use 100% and I won't now but basically, whatever the NRA is for, I'm against."

From Larry: "Thank goodness for the three second delay."

"Redding, California."

"What about healthcare?"

"My number one priority is to get health insurance for the almost fifty million Americans without it. My second priority will be to reduce fraud and other misdeeds from providers of medical services for Medicare and Medicaid. We will also review the business practices of insurance companies that provide services to government health programs."

From Larry: "An awful lot of folks are going to be upset with you."

"Larry, please. Number one, over a lifetime I've learned a lot about the people I mentioned and if it's helpful, I intend to use it. Number two, we both know and they know, my becoming President would be their worst nightmare and that's not likely to change."

"How much do you want to say about joining forces with Ms. Reinhardt?" Larry asked.

"She called. We talked at length, discovered we had similar value systems about the current political situation in America and the basis was formed for further discussion. Using logic and reason she convinced me I could run for office without engaging in politics as we know it. That I could say what I really believe. Based on the time we've spent together, I can say unequivocally, she's the most impressive person I've ever known."

"When I put together what you just said plus the impression she made on Ted Burner, we're talking about taking the human condition to extraordinary levels. She certainly impressed me. And now...drum roll, trumpet fanfare, absolute silence, and then this old man saying: Sam Saviur would you please tell your

73

friend why you think it's possible for a relatively unknown third party candidate to prevail against the two well funded major parties?"

"I'm really happy to put forth our take on the contest for the presidency of 2012 on a program hosted by MY friend. When we talk about what's best for this magnificent country the political positions and the candidates for both parties are not, I repeat not, relevant. I never thought I'd use this term about an American candidate for President but it fits. This guy on the right is just plain silly. I guess this shouldn't be surprising when you consider the group of candidates he came from. Interestingly, even if he were a formidable person it wouldn't make any difference. His party is known primarily for two characteristics:

Number 1. No matter the validity, the opinions of the American people, the brilliance of any proposal put forth by the administration, the conservatives block it or shoot it down. Behind these actions is the desire to make the president, not it's party but the president, look bad. They are pathological in their attempt to get him out of office. It's difficult to determine how much of their motivation comes from congressional members and how much comes from their frantic desire to please their financial backers and the wackos on the far right.

Number 2. When they originate a proposal for consideration, it's an asinine, once again silly budget proposal from this guy Lyan. I don't know where they dig up these people. Way back in the time of Reagan they had a fellow named Laffer, an excellent name. He proposed an innovative approach to our country's financial situation. The result? Nothing. More recently their bright shining star was Dick Stockman. Once again, zero results. To Mr. Stockman's credit: I've seen him on different TV programs within the last year or so. He's been decent enough to acknowledge flaws in his past pronouncements.

I believe our president has done a decent job but he has to deal with that wall I just described. As if that wasn't bad enough, I believe the same forces that spent almost a hundred million dollars to get Bill Clinton out of office are ready to spend whatever or do whatever to oust our current president."

"Do you believe race is a factor?"

"Without question. To sum it up, you have an impasse. On one side is the President and more or less, the Senate. On the other side we have the Conservative House of Representatives and their 'friends.' This does not bode well for our beloved country. More specifically, everyone knows we are in a global economy with China as our most dangerous rival. No one doubts our democracy is the best system of government on earth. However, while our impasse is so strong we were on the brink of shutting down the national government for a reason as simple as raising our debt ceiling, China's government can make financial and other types of decisions with global implications then move on them without delay. Not a good scenario.

While our people are busy maintaining their stalemate, the American electorate might be receptive to a clear, simple, common sense approach to getting our country back on track. Perhaps most important of all, should we be elected, there will be a lot of lobbyists looking for work. We will not be beholden to anyone and that standard will not change."

"As long as I've been around meeting people, getting their views, getting impressions, I can't assimilate what you've told me tonight into the world as I know it. Therefore, I don' t have a clue how far you and Ms. Reinhardt will go. I do wish you the very, very best. I used two verys because of that $10.00 maximum on contributions to your campaign."

"Thanks Larry. Can I send one more message?"

"Of course."

"I want to issue a challenge to every American eligible to vote: If you want a government whose only reason for existence is to be a positive factor in providing a good life for every American, who will not be influenced by special interests, who will listen and then act on your concerns, check us out.

Everything I've said tonight and every position we've taken on important problems facing America can be viewed on our web site,

'PatriciaAndSam.com'."

"Should you make it to the oval office do you have a specific plan on how you're going to get your legislation through congress and how you're going to break the stalemate you've mentioned?"

"I don't want to sound too corny, but no one promised me a rose garden. I know the challenges are monumental and you've described them well. And finally, as I say good evening, I do have a plan. Oh, I almost forgot. Chalk it up to inexperience. I would be willing to debate the two major candidates, with these conditions:

One on one

No moderator or audience

No time limits on questions or answers.

No incivility, meaning one individual talking at one time.

Now, good evening to all and so nice to spend some time with you, Larry."

CHAPTER 17

Knute Ginrich was having lunch with Delbert Gunnison, one of the more energetic and devoted members of the National Rifle Association. Delbert's political positions were so conservative they placed him considerably to the right of the late Jessie Yelms.

After the waiter left with their orders Knute said, "What's new in the wide open spaces of Idaho?"

"Same ol, same ol," replied Delbert. "I don't think I have to ask you the same question about your territory. That new guy on his white horse must be causing one hell of a lot of problems for you folks."

"We go back too far for me to play games with you Delbert. As if we didn't have enough problems with our candidate, that son of a bitch is the most dangerous threat I've ever seen, not only to our great Republican Party but to the United States of America. He just doesn't understand the ballgame and worse yet, as we sit here, I haven't come with an answer on how to handle him. There's been some pretty good boys that tried and came up empty.

CHAPTER 18

On the seventh of June, 2012, Delbert Gunnison spent a couple of hours with Rafe Ramsbottom tramping the woods behind Rafe's house some ten miles out of Lucile, Idaho. If you were standing right in the middle of downtown Lucile, you'd feel you were a long ways from anywhere. Ten miles out of Lucile and you wondered what the steady thumping sound was. Then you realized it was so quiet you were listening to the beating of your heart. There were absolutely no man made sounds except their voices and those caused by their movements. While rabbits were their primary quarry they would have shot at anything that moved.

The glue that held their relationship together was Rafe's ability as a marksman. Delbert was one of the best but Rafe stood alone. Even though they didn't have a great deal in common intellectually or socially, Delbert looked upon Rafe much like a high school quarterback would look upon Joe Montana.

Rafe had discovered during his military service in Vietnam that he initially enjoyed and then found he very much needed an enemy to fight. War, of course, was top of the line. Imagine being able to legally kill the most intelligent species on earth, your fellow human beings. Not only was it legal, but you were serving your country by doing it.

Like thousands of other Vietnam Veterans, Rafe was shocked by his reception upon returning home. He wasn't exactly expecting a hero's welcome but after the high of initial greetings by family and friends, he had grown increasingly bitter because of the lack of recognition given to him and his comrades by the government. This lack of recognition also applied to a large part of the American public. Rafe had come dangerously close to exploding on a couple of occasions but finally settled on distancing himself from people. Interestingly, he didn't allow his governmental rejection to dampen the patriotic fervor he felt for his country. In recent years, his battles consisted of contests of survival between him and all wild living creatures he could shoot in the vast uninhabited area around his ramshackle house.

Rafe felt somewhat honored by Delbert's interest in him as well as experiencing much needed ego gratification from Delbert's appreciation of his awesome accuracy, particularly with a rifle.

After completing what turned out to be a fruitless search for victims, Delbert and Rafe sat on the wooden steps leading to the front porch of Rafe's house and talked about the continuing lack of rain and related subjects. Delbert allowed that if the lack of rain wasn't bad enough in terms of the health of the surrounding wilderness and all of it's inhabitants, he was concerned about Sam Saviur's unbelievable standing in the race for the Presidency.

He told Rafe that he wouldn't put it past Saviur to try to declare a lot more land in their state to be National Parks. That would bring about immediate protection of all the birds and animals within these parks.

Delbert's gaze had been fixed on the unspoiled landscape. Had he been looking at Rafe's face, he first would have seen Rafe's eyes register excitement, then, almost immediately his entire face reflected the origin of resolve.

On Thursday, the 21st of June, 2012, Samuel Saviur stood some several feet from the small group that had traveled with him to this magnificent, beautiful area of western Idaho. Their purpose for going there was two-fold: To film footage that could be used in putting forth their views on environmental issues and to allow Sam a few days respite from the rigors of his campaign.

It was precisely 4:12 P.M. when a bullet fired from a high powered rifle shattered the brain stem of Sam Saviur. Death was instantaneous.

CHAPTER 19

When Patricia reviewed the events of the past thirty days, she was heartened by the acceptance of their campaign and could actually see the possibility of a victory in November. For one of the few times in her life, she was satisfied with her personal effort. There had been no blunders of importance and her overall strategy was succeeding beyond expectations. She couldn't help but smile and shake her head when she remembered the frustrations she felt as a Senator.

Patricia also knew her relationship with Sam had become a very important part of her life. The operative word here was respect. His focus on improving the lives of the American people was intense and inspirational. He never spoke about this process. He only talked of the specifics that could enable him to move forward and then took action. Because this effort permeated his entire existence, he tried to balance it with self-deprecation, usually expressed through humor. This was done because Sam believed his life's work made it impossible for him to develop other aspects of his personality. It was his way of trying to present an acceptable persona.

When Patricia thought of Sam in an overall sense she felt a warm glow.

The sound of the phone ringing seemed louder than normal because of Patricia's euphoria. She had barely said "hello" when she heard the words, "They've killed

Sam." Patricia didn't identify the caller and she didn't assimilate the rest of his message. She very carefully replaced the receiver and stood there, absolutely frozen.

Within a minute the phone rang again, and Patricia did not pick it up. She very slowly removed the plug from the side of the phone, then walked carefully to her rocking chair. She sat down without leaning back, clasped her hands together, then lowered them to her lap.

The severity of her shock was increased beyond measure because she had been so open, so vulnerable just a few seconds before hearing those three devastating words.

After a few minutes as her thought processes began to thaw, she tried denial. For Patricia this was a first. It was her nature to face everything in life head on.

When she began to accept the meaning of what she'd heard she felt herself beginning to black out. Somehow she remembered it helped to take slow, deep breaths when in periods of great stress. Concentrating on this function was a welcome distraction.

From the very beginning the possibility of Sam being harmed had been her worst fear. It grew stronger as she came to know and understand him. In this moment of crisis, she didn't think about what she was trying to accomplish for her country. She thought in terms of herself as one human being having been a party to affecting a terrible wrong on another.

Patricia began to undress as she headed for her shower. She didn't know why but her thought processes worked well in the shower. It had happened so often, she knew it wasn't coincidence.

After a few minutes of the water hitting her back with a force that almost hurt, she felt like she was able to once again begin functioning. Her father once told her to never make a decision when she was sick, tired or angry. Good advice but it had no application here. She had to make one of the biggest decisions of her life and she had to do it right now.

After a little while she knew that in fact, this was an easy decision. Since Sam had given his life for her idea the very least she could do was to go forward.

Whether or not the country was ready for a woman President didn't make a damn bit of difference. From any viewpoint, she had to replace Sam. There was no one who understood, who could articulate what their campaign was all about and then gain the acceptance of Sam's followers. Patricia, also instinctively, knew that the resolve and dedication necessary to finish what she and Sam had started was the best answer to her grief.

Such a response would not be difficult for her since it went well with her makeup. Because she had always been a front runner and Sam's death was the worst single thing that ever happened to her, she didn't' realize her capacity to fight for her beliefs.

If Sam's death was part of a plot to destroy their campaign, if "they" thought she'd panic and run, well "they" sure God had another think coming.

After drying off and wrapping herself in her robe, she plugged in the phone and called her father. She assured him that she was alright. She then explained that he didn't have to call his friends in Israel since she would be receiving Secret Service protection. This was a rather unusual way to tell her father she would become the candidate for President.

Finally, she told David her first two priorities were to choose a Vice President and then make a nationally televised speech. When her father asked her for her VP choice, she said Michael Boomberg. When David expressed strong doubts regarding her being able to get him, Patricia agreed, swore him to absolute secrecy, then on a whim, received her father's permission to use his jet and the lodge at Jackson Hole, Wyoming.

After their conversation had ended, David wondered why he had been so matter of fact about what was happening to the most important person in his life. Was it as simple as knowing and understanding Patricia? With a shrug of his shoulders he thought, most probably, yes.

Patricia called her secretary, thanked her for her condolences before she could offer them and suggested she hang loose for some turbulent times.

Patricia then called Ted Burner. His secretary said he was enroute to California and would call within ten minutes. Six minutes later, Patricia heard Burner say, "I'm sorry. I got word just a short time ago and tried to call. What can I do to help?"

"What's the best time for a nationally televised speech?"

"Nine P.M. Eastern. This brings it in a little early on the west coast but you're in good shape everywhere else."

"Can you schedule me for the twenty sixth?"

"Consider it done. Anything else?"

"Not right now, except I want you to know you're one hell of a friend, friend."

Burner smiled, and then told one of his aides to set up the broadcast.

Patricia called her secretary. "Call all of the usual media people. Tell them I will have absolutely no statement, nothing. They will hear from me on CNN the evening of the twenty sixth of June. Talk to you soon."

When Patricia reflected for a moment on her roller coaster ride over the last ninety minutes, she couldn't help but wonder what had fueled her remarkable recovery from a near breakdown to full speed ahead. One word flashed though her mind, anger. With all her remarkable faculties, Patricia, at that moment, didn't understand how this anger would forge a resolve and dedication that would carry her through to the conclusion of her mission.

CHAPTER 20

After the grief, shock and anger had lessened, Patricia decided to follow a practice she learned from her father. When David had to collect his thoughts and recharge his batteries, so to speak, he would go to his lodge just outside Jackson Hole, Wyoming. From every room the view of the Grand Tetons was breathtaking. Patricia shared her father's love of mountains and the Tetons were their favorites.

Having received David's permission she called the company operating the Gulfstream jet, gave them her destination and scheduled a pickup at Washington National for 7 PM that evening.

In the late afternoon after telling her secretary she would be out of town for forty eight hours, she packed a small bag, called a cab and within an hour, was on her way to the airport. Before boarding the plane she called Max. He lived at the lodge year round. He was a marvelous cook, kept the place immaculate and never missed meeting a flight with a smiling, cheerful welcome.

Patricia had planned to spend her time in the air working on her speech. She made good progress on the way west.

CHAPTER 21

When she stepped through the front door of the lodge, it was almost midnight, local time. She quickly changed to a very old, flannel night gown and thought she was mentally and physically exhausted to the point where falling asleep wouldn't be a problem. Didn't happen. So, she started method number one. It consisted of tightening her muscles for nine seconds then a quick release. Her starting point was the soles of her feet continuing through each section of her body and ending with her fingers. Five minutes later she was gone.

In the early morning, Patricia was awakened by the rather loud ringing of the phone. It was her secretary. "I called Sam's number one assistant. He said Sam's instructions indicated immediate cremation with the ashes being scattered at a location known only by the assistant. He also said that family notification did not apply. Patricia had always been aware of Elizabeth's competence but this action reached another level.

"What can I say except a heartfelt 'Thank you'."

"Happy to help. You take care of yourself."

"You do the same and once again, my thanks."

After splashing some very cold water on her face, Patricia went through her lodge arrival ritual. She didn't look out a window until she finished her favorite mini-breakfast of freshly ground, strong Columbian coffee, black, accompanied by a 'just out of the oven' croissant with butter and ollalieberry jam. Only then did she draw the curtains covering a large bay window. She looked at the improbable Tetons then began to cry. Going from the horror of yesterday to the beauty before her was too much, even for a person as strong as Patricia. She then went to the nearest mirror, looked at herself and said out loud, "Turn off the water works, lady. Long ways to go and a short time to get there." She then went into the bathroom and began the mechanics of morning.

After changing into her favorite, well worn sweatsuit she did her almost daily two miles of light jogging then returned to her 'Jackson Hole' rocking chair armed with pen and pad. Prior to her beginning work, she called her father. Before he could ask she told him she was weepy but alright. She then said, "Tell me about Michael Boomberg."

"He's one of us but he plays the game so well, you'd never know it. He's also very fast when it comes to him accomplishing his objectives. Finally, he's straightforward and to the point, quickly."

"Sounds like my hunch is pretty close. Thanks, take care."

David barely got out a "Bye."

CHAPTER 22

Patricia thought about the timing on her call to Boomberg and decided the sooner the better. While dialing the main number of the New York City mayor's office, Patricia couldn't help but smile. With all her connections, here she was dialing the number she received from information. The operator answered. "Hello, this is Patricia Reinhardt. May I please talk to Mayor Boomberg?" Within thirty seconds, the mayor was on the line. "Ms. Reinhardt, I'm terribly sorry about Sam."

"Thank you, Mr. Mayor. Please accept my apology for the short notice but could you include me on Monday's schedule? I'm about to make one of the most important decisions of my life and I'd like to talk to you about the possibility of your involvement."

"What's your starting point on Monday?"

"Jackson Hole, Wyoming. I'm using my father's plane."

"Late afternoon would be best for me. If you can set up a departure getting you into the New York area mid-afternoon, that should work. David and I use the same company so I'll have no problem getting your arrival time. Tell the crew to go into Newark and park at the executive terminal. Look for a black Cadillac SUV. Mary will be the driver and she'll be close to the aircraft. She will drive you to the garage of my apartment building and escort you to my place."

In a soft voice reflecting relief, she didn't have a second choice for V.P., gratitude, and the emotional stress of the last twenty four hours, Patricia said, "thank you. Look forward to our meeting."

"See you on Monday. Safe trip." After reflecting on the short conversation, Michael couldn't remember any response, ever, that was so out of character. Not one question? But then, what can you do with a damsel in distress? Based on the sound of Ms. Reinhardt's last words, there could be no doubt about the level of this distress. Also, Michael, did the beauty and persona of the caller come into play?"

CHAPTER 23

On the flight west, Patricia had made good progress on her speech. She tried to continue but all of her thoughts seemed tired and ordinary. She sighed and decided to take a long look at the Tetons hoping it would jumpstart a flow of words.....nothing. She went into the kitchen for a bottle of water.

On the way back to her rocking chair she noticed, on an end table, a DVD of the movie Secretariat. Secretariat was one of the greatest race horses, ever. Someone had told her it was worth viewing. Since she had grown up around horses, that opinion was reason enough to ask Max to pick up a copy on one of his trips into town. Maybe a little diversion would get her back on track. Besides, it was based on the true story of a very impressive woman, Penny Chenery. Patricia was always in a 'learning mode', which meant she listened carefully to whatever communication she received. Communication could mean conversation with a friend up to a lecture from a renowned educator and everything in between. Accordingly, she didn't miss much of Secretariat's dialogue. This didn't require much effort since it was such a welcome change from the last couple of weeks in addition to being an excellent movie.

When you add Patricia's 'listening' to her being precocious, in terms of the human condition, plus her hobby of people watching, it was a slam dunk to understand three primary characteristics of the main character, put forth brilliantly by the lead actor, Diane Lane.

Intuition told her that Secretariat possessed qualities of greatness. It was also a factor in choosing the right trainer. The owner of the horse considered Secretariat's chief rival said of her 'Intuition can only take her so far.' Right. Far enough for her horse to win the Triple Crown.

Strength of character was the major factor in her refusing to sell her father's horse farm despite extreme pressure from her husband and brother. She was also strong enough to turn down a multi-million offer to buy Secretariat.

Her sensitivity enabled her to have major disagreements with her trainer and jockey then reconsider and develop a positive relationship with both of them. It also was an important factor in facing the difficulties of balancing her responsibilities as a mother and wife with the monumental effort of taking Secretariat to the absolute pinnacle of horse racing.

CHAPTER 24

To this point in her life, Patricia had spent most of her time in a world of men. With the ever-present exceptions, she could say that at least ninety percent of these men did not have the qualities of Ms. Tweedy (In the movie, the owner of Secretariat was known by that name.). That explained her disappointments in the movers and shakers passing through her father's house in her younger years. It also explained her frustrations and disillusionment with her make colleagues that led to her resigning from the senate. If these people had just one of these qualities, character, lack of intellectual integrity wouldn't be so common.

While she had been aware of many women with these qualities over the years, Patricia found it hard to accept she had never established the difference, as determined by these qualities, between men and women. In her defense, she had been so busy setting, then achieving goals, there wasn't much time left for other pursuits. Also, clouding any such discovery were the high number of women who, in their desire to 'get into the game' adopted the behavior of men. Ms. Tweedy maintained the integrity of her true nature, woman, with a capital W.

They say that necessity is the mother of invention. While the response to Sam's candidacy, based on the number of $10.00 contributions had been positive, there was no indication of any breakthrough with the 'silent ones', those who chose not to participate in the election process. Was it just a matter of time and the message sinking in or was it back to the drawing board?

When Patricia reconsidered, again, the qualities Ms Tweedy put forth in Secretariat, she decided to self-evaluate and determine how many applied to her. No question reguarding sensitivity and intuition, but then almost all women have these two, if they're true to their nature. While she felt it would be presumptuous to evaluate her character, she did know that determination was part of her makeup.

While Patricia was still shaking her head about not realizing these terrific qualities indigenous to most women, she thought about the ridiculous position women occupied in American business and government. Three percent of Fortune 500 companies CEOs are women. Women still earn seventy seven cents to every dollar men make, for the same work. Just eighteen percent of the U.S. Congress are women. The U.S. ranks 90th among the countries of the world in terms of women in high government positions. How could all this be happening when most women possessed qualities so desperately needed in such troubled times?

The status of American women seemed particularly unfair when she revisited her thoughts on the movie. If Ms. Tweedy could succeed at the highest level in a male dominated sport and/or business such as horse racing, that would indicate she could do well in the environments of business and government on any level. With all due respect due Ms Tweedy, it would then follow logically that there were many women who could emulate her. This was true since all the important qualities required were really part of a woman's nature. For women to use these qualities, the only requirement was living by the words of William Shakespeare, 'To thine own self be true'. The importance of this standard could not be stated too strongly. Doing otherwise such as adopting the characteristics of men, would render useless their inherent qualities. You're being redundant, Patricia. From that point, Patricia's mind moved so quickly it was difficult to maintain any order. Even with this torrent of thoughts she knew her next step was a major revision of the speech content begun on the flight to Jackson Hole.

With her writer's block gone, Patricia had to slow her writing to insure its legibility.

CHAPTER 25

Except for a night of tossing and turning in a futile attempt for sustained sleep, Patricia worked continuously. By late afternoon on Sunday she had her speech covered. Some was in final form; the rest could be completed on the flight to Newark.

While working, Patricia did reasonably well trying to cope with her grief. As soon as she stopped she burst into tears. Her only recourse was a valiant and moderately successful attempt to effect a mental block.

Rather than rocking and crying as she looked at the Tetons, Patricia decided to go into town for dinner at Vitos, her favorite restaurant anywhere. She called Vito, accepted his condolences for a short time then requested that he and the rest of the very nice people who worked there to please put a hold on what she knew were their heartfelt feelings. She also asked if her secluded booth was available, received a quick 'yes' then said she would have the 'usual'. That meant angel hair pasta topped by a small amount of plain marinara sauce and her version of a terrific antipasto. The antipasto would have just the right amount of Italian meats and cheese, room temperature, accompanied by garbanzo beans, pepperoncini, olives, etc and the right blend of olive oil and wine vinegar. She also said yes to a carafe of the house red, a wine so smooth you just didn't realize how much was going down.

Since Patricia's normal intake of alcohol was an occasional glass of wine, usually with lunch or dinner, enjoying all the contents of the carafe caused her to travel at a reduced rate of speed back to the lodge. After a short conversation with a crew member it was determined that a 9 AM departure would allow a 3 PM touchdown at the airport in Newark. Patricia asked Max for a 7:30 AM wake up, an 8:00 breakfast and an 8:30 out of the driveway to the airport.

Two hours of quality time on her speech, an hour on her meeting with the mayor along with intermittent dozing and Patricia had just enough time to freshen up before the beginning of the descent for landing.

CHAPTER 26

The sleek Gulfstream taxied up to the Newark executive terminal at 3:10 PM. This was a good arrival time from an air traffic standpoint. Patricia thanked the pilot, co-pilot and flight attendant, told them to stand by for a departure to Washington within three hours, then she carefully descended the extended steps and walked briskly to the black SUV parked some fifty yards away.

While Mary was cordial she apparently was operating under instructions to speak when spoken to. Patricia appreciated the quiet time since it allowed a review of her notes on the meeting with the mayor.

No traffic delays on the New Jersey turnpike, the normal madness in Manhattan but Mary's effortless handling of the SUV and the route she chose effected a 4:00 PM arrival at the mayor's apartment building located on the Upper East Side.

Mary escorted Patricia to the door of Boomberg's apartment, pressed a button, said goodbye and walked to the elevator. In less than a minute the door opened and a smiling mayor with hand extended was a few feet away from Patricia. Warm handshake then, "Please come in." Patricia was somewhat surprised at the mayor's casual attire. Loafers, Levi's, golf shirt and v-necked sweater. He led her to his study, motioned to a comfortable looking couch, then sank into a large chair behind his desk.

"How about a drink? Something to eat?"

"I'm good to go."

"I would appreciate you calling me Michael. Your preference?"

"Patricia."

"Now tell me about your important decision and my possible involvement."

"I'm going to announce my candidacy for president tomorrow evening and I'd like you to join me as V.P."

"Why me?"

"1. Money, for sure, and power, probably would not be motivations.

2. In terms of real vocational capacity, I'm guessing you're currently around fifty percent."

3. You could be a little tired being mayor of New York City.

4. The thought of operating at the top of our national government might appeal to you.

5. Your very smart and you get things done, quickly.

6. You're a warrior.

7. You've been a 'mover and a shaker'.

From Michael, a blink, then, "How much of what you just said is you and how much is your father?"

"I rarely say one hundred percent so, ninety eight percent me. My father's main contribution was confirmation of some of what I just told you."

"Why do you think you can win? You, and, I'm so sorry, Sam, were doing well but still had a long way to go."

"After tomorrow's speech I believe you'll see the beginnings of a move....upward. Here's why: What happened to Sam has given me the fuel to start and finish a campaign that will have no precedence. It will be a calm measured attack on the forces that have put America in a very dangerous position in terms of it's future. It will also put forth what I would do to reduce this danger and put this magnificent country on a path of sustained progress. From a third party viewpoint: For what I have in mind, the timing is perfect, i.e. you'd have to go way back to find a time when the American public has had so little respect for both major parties. If this lack of leadership wasn't bad enough, we also have the gridlock in Washington making movement in any direction impossible. Moving right along, may I present potential third party members, the millions upon millions of women, who, for the most part, have stood by and accepted indignities of a magnitude that's difficult to comprehend. Talk about motivated voters! There has been a war on women and I'll fly a few drones over that one. I'll also put forth some sad info on the current status of women. I really intend to clobber the people in both political parties and the business world. I haven't decided whether to do a number on our pathetic supreme court.

Finally, I'll tell women and men who understand, they have qualities that make them better qualified for leadership than most of the men currently in positions of power and or leadership.

Why their inherent qualities regarding leadership are desperately needed in America, right now.

You're the first person that's heard that from me since I first realized it in Jackson Hole. Have you seen the movie, Secretariat? "

"Yes."

"Does it make sense that Ms. Tweedy's qualities, sensitivity, intuition and character were main contributors to her astounding accomplishments?"

"Yes, got the picture, pun intended. Why did it take you so long to understand that women have these impressive, inherent qualities?"

"Good question. Starting in my teens I began setting goals and then working very hard to reach them. I was also distracted by all those women who have decided to emulate men in their attempt to get into the game."

"It's been quite a while since I've listened for such a long period of time. Please accept my compliments on the quality of your presentation and your interesting ideas. Now, give me your concept of the vice-president's position in your administration."

"You would be the most powerful V.P. in American history. We would work as a team and your power within the administration would be a smidgen below mine. We would decide how many people we need to pursue our goals and choose them together. These goals would be:

A national energy policy

Enhancing our position as a world power though economics instead of military.

Examining our military effort worldwide along with the military-industrial complex, with cost reductions as our major consideration.

The Bowles-Simpson report will set the guidelines for an all out effort toward stabilizing, then moving forward with regards to America's economy.

Providing health insurance for the fifty million Americans without it.

Enacting legislation that would provide effective, meaningful regulation of our financial community.

Enhancing the government's ability to minimize wrongdoing on the part of all providers of services to the federal government. Particular emphasis will be placed on those providing medical services.

A national overhaul of grades K through 12 in our educational system.

Establishing a high priority for long term financing of social security, medicare and Medicaid.

I know your approach toward working on the areas I've prioritized would be straightforward, no nonsense and tough. If I didn't believe what I just said I wouldn't be talking to you. When anyone from the opposition insults our intelligence, they will pay a price and it won't be pleasant. We will not be reaching across the aisle unless the people on the other side have their hand out and they mean it. If we work well together and you want to run for President in 2016, I'll step aside. Any questions? "

"Yes. I can see you winning the presidency but how about those 'just say no' people when we try to get our legislation through congress?"

"I don't have any illusions about winning enough house and senate seats to control congress. I do think we'll win enough in both legislative areas to make it very interesting. Now I'll make it very, very interesting and say one word that will be a game changer....coalition."

From Michael, a smile, then, "No further questions." He handed Patricia a card and said "Call me at this number when you get back to your place and I'll give you my answer. Just one comment. I have a feeling a lot of movers and shakers will be doing a lot more shaking after they hear your speech. Mary will be waiting in the lobby. She'll take you back to the airport or wherever. "

When Michael opened the door, Patricia said, "Thanks for your time Michael." She then extended her hand. Michael put both of his hands around Patricia's and in a soft voice said, "My not commenting on what you've said means nothing, except now and then I just want to listen. Good night." Patricia looked into Michael's eyes and said, "Good night."

CHAPTER 27

For some considerable period of time after Patricia left, Michael sat in his chair and re-examined his belief that he had seen and done it all. I mean, what could be new to a billionaire mayor of New York City? He had agreed to meet with Patricia for two reasons: sincere and heartfelt compassion for the effect of Sam Saviur's death on Patricia combined with wanting to see her up close. Rather than the standard man-woman motivation Michael's was more like a collector of paintings. When she was in his presence, he found her visually flawless. Then, the impact of her words was as strong as that of her beauty.

Michael took great pride in his agile, quick, imaginative mind. He was therefore shocked that he could never conjure up a scenario where this woman, or for that matter, any person, could walk into his life and in less than an hour present a perspective that was new. Not only was it new, he was in complete agreement with everything she put forth.

He had never known a fellow mover and shaker, and they were all men, who wasn't motivated by money, power and/or status. This motivation was so strong, they failed or refused to recognize the harm their actions brought to their country and it's people. This Reinhardt woman had presented him with an opportunity that would be his most difficult, exciting challenge, ever. If he succeeded he could improve the life quality of millions upon millions of people. In specific numbers it would be a multiple of forty times the population of New York City.

Michael wasn't thinking about payback for past transgressions. He honestly believed that a grading system for integrity, based on a curve, would place him in the top three percent of his fellow heavy hitters. What made the whole thing so absolutely mind boggling was the fact that he truly wanted to move on. Had he spent a month in seclusion trying to come up with something specific and utterly sensational he wouldn't have come close to Patricia's offer. Worst case, even if they lost, he would have left his job as mayor for good and sufficient reason.

CHAPTER 28

Two minutes after Patricia walked through the door of her condo she dialed Michael's number.

"Hello, Patricia, or should I say hello, boss."

Big sigh of relief. Then, "Thanks for the quick response. I'll do my very best to make your decision a good one."

"I know you will. Two questions. If we win and I decide to give it a go in 2016, will you be my V.P.? Also, do you want me to appear tomorrow evening?"

"Yes, on both. You probably know the time from all the spots they've been running and the place is the CNN studios in Washington."

"I'll be there at 8:30."

"Look forward and Michael, once again, thank you. Good night.

"Thank you Patricia, Good night."

CHAPTER 29

The largest television audience in American political history saw a Patricia Reinhardt who projected the quintessential steel fist in a velvet glove. She was composed, determined, and despite the trauma, anguish and lack of sleep over a seventy two hour period, she was beautiful beyond description.

Then, without introduction or a "good evening" she began. "I believe the American people have lost their best friend, ever. I asked him to run for president because he was a decent, hard working person who really cared about the people of this country. He possessed a brilliant mind that was focused on the big picture, the best interests of all Americans. For all of his adult life, he tried to serve those interests more than anyone I've ever known and he did this with an integrity factor that most people don't even understand, let alone appreciate. And now he's gone and I accept responsibility for his passing. I'm the one who convinced him that he could do more for his country as President than as a consumer advocate. I know there are those who figured I'd cut and run after Sam's death and I almost did. Not out of fear for my safety....because I was sick to the bottom of my soul.

Well, I'm not running away. I AM running for the Presidency. Now that I'm a candidate, American voters should know as much as possible about me. By giving you this information you'll understand the basis for my beliefs on the current status of our beloved country.

At age nine I became a confirmed people watcher. From my peers on up I wanted to learn what these folks were really thinking and feeling. I lived at my father's ranch in Rawlins, Wyoming until leaving for college. The ranch was a great place to watch and listen to people I referred to as movers and shakers. In other words, they were well known leaders in American government, business and education. Politicians and educators were interested in my father's fund raising capabilities. Businessmen sought his counsel regarding their strategies. While I expected and wanted to be favorably impressed, that was not the case. The impressions I received in that timeframe continued through my undergraduate years, law school and my terms as mayor and US Representative. I then received my Ph.D. in negative characteristics of male leaders as the junior U.S. Senator from Wyoming.

More specifically, the common thread running through my impressions in all the stages just listed, with the normal few exceptions, was a distinct lack of character. With this lack of character came intellectual dishonesty. These people knew what they were doing was wrong but they had elevated rationalization to a level difficult to comprehend. Not withstanding what I've just said I was surprised and horrified when we went into two wars because of the arrogance, stupidity and deception practiced by a group of fatally flawed movers and shakers. I wasn't surprised with the near meltdown of our financial system in 2008. Once again just chalk it up to our little movers and shakers doing their thing. More recently we've witnessed gridlock in our national legislative process brought about by our elected officials in Washington. While we're standing still our number one adversary, China, is moving, world-wide, particularly in the economic area.

On the day of Sam's assassination, with the hope it might help, I "ran away" to my father's lodge. It was built with the idea of providing spectacular views of the Grand Tetons mountain range. I was just as miserable there as I would have been in Washington. The day after my arrival, on nothing more than a whim I watched the movie "Secretariat". It was the incredible but true story of how a horse named Secretariat reached the pinnacle of horse racing by winning three races referred to as the triple crown. A woman named Penny Chenery was the force behind this amazing achievement. In my opinion she was a force because she followed the advice of William Shakespeare, 'To thine own self be true.' By doing this she brought into play three qualities that are inherent in most women; sensitivity, intuition, and character. Her intuition told her Secretariat possessed qualities of greatness. It was also a factor in her choosing an unusual trainer. Her sensitivity was a major factor in balancing her responsibilities as a mother and wife with the monumental effort to take her horse to the top.

Her strength of character caused her to stand up to extreme pressure from her brother and husband to sell her father's horse farm after his passing. She was also strong enough to refuse a multi-million dollar offer from a man who wanted to buy Secretariat.

After my earlier description of America's leaders it should come as no surprise when I say they don't do well in terms of sensitivity, intuition and character. Occasionally I do hear a man say 'That decision came from my gut'. Then there's the unforgettable remark of George W. Weed, 'I looked into Putin's eyes and saw his soul'. I mean, if he could see the Russian leader's soul, his possibilities are unlimited.

On a more serious note, watching 'Secretariat' made me realize, for the first time, this country has been wasting a valuable resource....women. If they're true to their nature, almost all of them have the big three. If more of our current and past leaders had these qualities we wouldn't be up to our necks in trouble.

So, what is the status of this valuable resource? Not good. That well known 'We've come a long way baby' only had merit because we started so low. Where are we right now? Three percent of all the Fortune 500 CEOs are women. Eighteen percent of the U.S. Congress are women. Women still make seventy-seven cents for every dollar men make, for the same work. Women in America rank 90th in the world in terms of high government positions. I mean...the women of LIBERIA forced a terrible leader out of office and took over the country.

If you have any doubts about the 'war on women', forget them. It is REAL. The drive to ban abortion completely is as strong as ever. There's even controversy about contraception. This war is being waged primarily by men. If you put all these guys together they wouldn't have the sensitivity of a bull moose in mating season. I won't compare their character to a moose. I don't want to insult the moose.

Personally, I question if they believe in their ridiculous pronouncements. They're so busy frantically dancing to the tune of those people way, way out there they don't have to use their minds. Not that it would make a difference.

Once again, to women and those men who understand, get out and vote for every qualified woman with a capital W. I'm talking from the local level on up to the federal and all the elections in between. If you believe you have the qualities to serve your constituents on whatever level, give it a go. For the best interests of our country as well as our personal interests we have to SMASH THAT GLASS CEILING. I'm sure there are many, many viewers surprised or even shocked at how strong and how direct my remarks have been. Well, unusual circumstances require unusual reactions. Anyone evaluating the America of 2012 honestly and objectively would have to consider the following:

America is facing several serious problems. Some examples:

An educational system that isn't working

High unemployment

A staggering national debt

Lack of an energy policy that forces us to deal with unstable countries in a part of the world that could explode at any time.

An approach to healthcare where costs are soaring out of sight and 50 million Americans have no health insurance.

We have operated under a patriarchal system since the beginning of our country so men must bear total responsibility for our problems. Even if women were only half as capable as I know they are we couldn't do any worse than the men. I'm not suggesting that women take over our country. I am recommending that we participate in all areas of our society commensurate with the number of women in America and their capabilities. Men are not going to change for the better unless they're faced with serious competition. Based on everything I've said tonight, women can be that competition. Finally, may I introduce my candidate for Vice President."

Patricia stands and Michael walks to a point just a few feet away from her.

"I've chosen Mr. Boomberg for two reasons: Number one, as you've heard this evening, I have been severely critical of our country's movers and shakers. I know, should I win in November, we will begin as adversaries. I do not want to contribute to the poisoned, polarized atmosphere so prevalent throughout the land. So, from day one, these people will be dealing directly with someone they know. They will also be talking to an individual who understands where they're coming from.

Number two, I believe Mr. Boomberg' credentials in business and government are exceptional. Accordingly, he will be the most powerful vice-president in the history of America. Michael?"

"Good evening. I have submitted my resignation as mayor of New York City effective September 15, 2012. The letter of resignation was delivered today."

I was aware of and in complete agreement with all of Ms. Reinhardt's remarks. For me, coming to this conclusion was not difficult since I have been a strong advocate of logic and reason for many years. Both of these words apply to everything she said.

Have I ever heard Ms. Reinhardt's case before? Going all the way back to my college days of course, I've heard bits and pieces, here and there. I have never heard such a summation from a businessman or a politician.

Once again, America needs, desperately women with a capital W. Also, watch and listen carefully when you get your copy of Secretariat. Thanks for your time and a pleasant evening to all of you. Ms. Reinhardt?"

"Our platform putting forth our positions on all national matters of importance can be viewed on our web site, Patricia.com, beginning at 8:00 AM eastern time tomorrow morning.

A few announcements: The Freedom Party will not have a national organization. There also will not be anyone calling you every five minutes. If you want to help your country and yourself, on election day, go to the designated location and cast your ballot.

I invite my two opponents to a one on one discussion. No moderator, no audience, no time limits on asking or answering questions and no incivility. By incivility I mean more than one person talking at a time. The location is open for negotiation.

For a complimentary DVD of 'Secretariat', no shipping or handling charges, email your request and mailing address to patricia.com. This offer is effective July 7, 2012.

Mr Boomberg will be available for interviews and appearances effective September 16, 2012. I am available immediately. All requests by email to patricia.com.

Barring unforeseen or unusual circumstances, my next national address will be on election eve. Good night and good luck.

CHAPTER 30

Michael and Patricia met in what TV people refer to as the Green Room.

"I knew you moved quickly once you made a decision, Michael, but two examples in twenty four hours? Impressive."

"I try to keep media exposure to a minimum and in this particular instance there was only one way to play it. Speaking of the media, my car, with Mary at the wheel, is positioned so we can leave the area nonstop. Can I give you a lift to your place?"

"You said the magic words. I'll try to stay awake until I give her directions."

As Patricia left the SUV she hoped her words were "Call you tomorrow."

CHAPTER 31

The next morning, Patricia was awakened by a call from her father. After her sleepy but warm greeting David suggested she return his call when he could understand what she was saying.

"Good work on getting Michael. Since you'll be going after the movers and shakers, having one of the best on your side is a real plus. Anything interesting on why you were successful....besides your persuasive powers?"

"Not really. He'll have unprecedented power for a V.P. It's a much bigger challenge than mayor of New York. And he agrees with my target areas. Also, while he didn't say it, running New York City could be wearing a little thin."

"I know you're aware of this but I'll say it anyway. After all, one of the main functions of a father is protecting his offspring against major mistakes. Will he be tough enough in cases where he'll be coming down on his friends?"

"Based on how I read Michael, he knows how strongly I feel about slowing these guys. I'm reasonably sure he would not have accepted my offer if he intended to go easy."

On another subject, with the usual few exceptions, I don't trust the media. Should I require a tape covering the entirety of my interviews along with the right to publicize them at my discretion?"

"Based on my experience with these people, excellent idea.

"Thanks Dad, love you."It was always so nice talking to her father. She wondered why she didn't call more often.

CHAPTER 32

Mr. Omama refused to debate.

After a long meeting with his top advisors, candidate Konmey concluded that he had no choice but to debate Patricia, on her terms. No notes or moderator, each would ask the other questions with no time limit on answers and civility would be the order of the day, i.e. only one person talking at a time.

With his running well behind Patricia in the polls, plus the surge caused by her recent speech and Boomberg joining her campaign, he knew he was in big trouble. While it was unlikely that even a decisive victory in the debate would rescue him, there was always the possibility that she would make a mistake. A mistake so monumental that he would have at least a chance.

While all of Komney's advisors except one agreed that he had nothing to lose, his wife, Alice, was against the debate. She said nothing in public but made her view crystal clear in private conversations with her husband. When he asked for her reasoning, she was startlingly vague. For someone who always expressed herself in a very direct, clear manner, all she could offer was a feeling of foreboding. A feeling so dark and so strong that it transcended the contest for the Presidency.

The one exception among Konmey's advisors was more specific than Mrs. Konmey on why he shouldn't debate Patricia. She had believed for some time that he had a strong repression problem when it came to attractive women. She had seen too many quick but meaningful looks going their way along with that same look when greeting a good looking woman. Finally, his body language when talking to a pretty woman was distinctly different as compared to a conversation with a man, or a woman with ordinary looks.

She also knew, that Komney didn't understand that Patricia, when it came to feminine appeal, was in a class all her own.

The debate was held in an auditorium on the campus of Georgetown University. The stage, some four feet above the floor, was framed by a floor to ceiling dark blue curtain. The only objects on this stage were a small wooden table that held a pitcher of ice water and two glasses.

Konmey had never met Patricia, nor had he ever seen her in person, until she was walking towards him thirty seconds before air time.

She smiled, extended her right hand and said, "Good evening, Mr Konmey."

Of the millions watching, only a small number would notice Konmey's blink and the slight hesitation before extending his hand and returning Patricia's greeting.

At exactly 9:00 PM the announcer explained the debate's format. He then said that Patricia had won the coin toss attended by the participant's representatives just a few minutes before nine and she would ask the first question.

"Mr. Konmey, in Webster's Seventh New Collegiate Dictionary under 'Character' is the phrase 'The complex of mental and ethical traits marking a person, group or nation.' Describe your version of the ideal President in terms of this definition, then evaluate yourself, using your description as the standard."

Konmey had spent hours preparing to discuss his position on issues, particularly those put forth by Patricia. For example, he had given a high priority to fashioning a response to a question he was sure Patricia would ask, 'Why hadn't he emphasized the need for a strong energy policy?'

While he remembered clearly her castigation of the movers and shakers in government and business, he felt that Patricia would not bring up the character issue. He had no understanding of why he had come to this conclusion because it was part of his pathetic attempt to convince himself that Patricia was just another political opponent.

Subconsciously, he also played a mind game indicating Patricia had too much respect for the Presidency to confront him on that issue. Besides, anyone that beautiful would be too nice to go for the jugular.

Jimmy Barter once stated that he had on occasion felt lust in his heart. As Konmey stood there trying to fashion a response to Patricia's opening remarks, he felt lust in every part of his body. Its effect was especially devastating since he had intentionally blocked out the effect Patricia might have on him.

The combination of this lust and the surprise of Patricia's first question caused a virtual 'red out' in his thought processes. As a result, the normally glib, fast on his feet Konmey could only stammer and ask Patricia to repeat the question. Upon hearing it a second time he began to answer along the lines of an open mind and the highest ethical standards.

The realization that all of his Presidential chips were on the table sent Konmey over the edge. The TV audience could hear him say, in a strained voice, "Asking questions of a personal nature is not presidential. Your lack of…..experience…". Then he started to cry. As tears rolled down his cheeks a member of his staff rushed out, faced the cameras and said, "The cumulative strain of the primaries plus that of the campaign has been too much for Mr. Konmey. Please accept our apologies." With his arms around Konmey's shaking shoulders, Konmey was led away from center stage.

Patricia had been standing there with a look of genuine concern. As the staff member and Konmey left, she said, "I wish Mr. Konmey a speedy recovery and hope our debate can be re-scheduled in the near future. Good evening." The cameras followed her exit until she left the stage.

CHAPTER 33

Two days after the 'debate', Patricia received a call from Mrs. Omama asking for a meeting. Mrs. Omama did not specify the reason for her request. Patricia quickly agreed. After a short discussion it was determined that Patricia could arrive at the White House in the late evening thereby minimizing the chances of discovery by the media.

Mrs. Omama explained her request for the meeting within the first few minutes following Patricia's arrival. "I've been trying for a long time to reach my version of success in terms of my efforts as a mother, wife and traveler on the fast track. It's my opinion that I'm not doing very well. Even with all the advantages of my position, I'm always looking for advice regarding this effort. Based on what I know about you, I felt you have the capability to produce some pearls of wisdom in that area. If my definition of having it all is satisfaction in the three areas I've mentioned, do you believe it's possible?"

"No, it isn't. This applies to men as well as women. Men are able to create the illusion of having it all because women pick up so much of the slack."

Even with exceptional time management, a twenty four hour day isn't long enough. By the time you meet the requirements of your vocational effort, by the time you eat, sleep, take care of personal grooming, travel and dispense with all the minutiae of daily living, it isn't possible from just the standpoint of simple mathematics, i.e. dividing overall effort into the hours available.

Just as compelling are the limitations of our abilities to switch gears mentally. If you've had a great day vocationally, it's hard to come down from the high you're on and concentrate on family. If you've had a bad day, it's hard to come up.

In addition to the emotional, you have the problem of closing off the myriad of thoughts that are constantly flashing through our minds. Then there's the quality of your personal relationships. Any fluctuation adds to the problem. I realize I've offered a capsulization but I'm sure you can round it out."

"What do you think of my husband?"

"I'm going to use a word that's been entering my thoughts lately. Timing."

"How does that come into your opinion of my husband?"

"As you well know we're going through a mean, vicious, polarized period within our country's political system. Your husband's being so nice is a negative in this atmosphere. He's also too cautious."

"No questions on the nice part but give me an example of 'too cautious'."

"This is my personal belief. He should have issued an order bringing our troops home from Afghanistan and Iraq within thirty days of his inauguration. I can explain my position in detail but I know you're a very busy lady and I'll save that for another day. Other than those two examples I believe he's been a good

President and may I say you've been a terrific First Lady.

"Thank you. On the subject of being nice, that description certainly fits you. Can you deal with the atmosphere you've described?"

"Yes I can. I am ready."

"I appreciate your quick response to my request for a meeting."

"No problem. I'm certainly not clairvoyant but after talking to you I have the impression you're about to come to an important decision. Whatever the case, I certainly wish you and your lovely family the very best."

"Thanks again. I'll walk you to the door."

"Thank you. I've enjoyed meeting you and that's not a political remark."

The first lady, smiling, said "You're very kind, good night."

"Good night."

CHAPTER 34

On Friday the 27th of July, 2012, the following statement was issued from the White House:

For reasons associated with the well being and safety of my family I will conclude my candidacy for President of the United States, effective immediately. I will provide my services as required for transition to the new candidate. I will also continue to serve as President until the inauguration of the incoming President in January, 2013. There will be no further statements.

Everyone from the President's closest confidantes to those in the country old enough to understand were simply stunned.

Twenty four hours after the announcement the world's media reaction consisted of nothing more than speculation. The only individuals with any meaningful information were Mr. and Mrs. Omama and possibly their two children.

EPILOGUE

Within thirty days after becoming available, over seven million DVDs were mailed, eighty percent to women and a surprising twenty percent to men.

None of the media requesting interviews objected to providing a tape and giving Patricia the right to publicize any differences regarding content. They also agreed to review previous interviews so repetition of questions would be minimized.

A few sidelights on Patricia's early interviews: She placed a 'zero colorful' language condition on Bill Raher's request. He quickly agreed.

On Betterman she was asked to give an opinion on Konmey. Her answer: Based on their brief debate along with watching the parade of would-be candidates through the primaries of his party, she believed every candidate for President should undergo a psychiatric evaluation.

When asked about the governor of New Jersey becoming Vice President, Patricia said he shouldn't be considered without a substantial weight loss. Millions of obese Americans were in need of positive examples. Also coming into play, that old, but valid, 'the VP is a heartbeat away from the Presidency'. The Governor's weight problem certainly presents serious health implications. Patricia agreed to an interview with Greta Cistern of Fox News thereby sending Bill O'Smiley into orbit.

By choosing wisely plus judicious spacing of interviews Patricia and later Boomberg were almost continuously before the public, visually or in print or on radio.

On election eve Patricia gave a five minute summation of her first speech. She reminded American voters their first priority was actually casting their ballot. They should also use their hearts AND their minds in making their choice.

With Konmey's collapse and Omama's withdrawl plus an angry, frustrated electorate, Patricia won by five points. The Freedom Party also had moderate success in winning several seats in the House and Senate. Most of the newcomers were women.

On December 1, 2012, Patricia and Boomberg met with the highest ranking members of one of the major parties. After several hours, both sides agreed they had enough in common to meet again. All involved saw a distinct possibility of their combined votes having a positive effect in moving the National Legislature out of its' prolonged stalemate.

At Patricia's inauguration, when it was time for her to place her hand on the bible, there was a slight delay. John Noberts, the chief justice of the Supreme Court had to kneel and pick up the bible he dropped after looking into the eyes of the most beautiful President in America's history.

www.ingramcontent.com/pod-product-compliance
Lightning Source LLC
Chambersburg PA
CBHW060127260626
47160CB00005B/2041